War Girl Series
Book 4

Marion Kummerow

**Trouble Brewing**

Marion Kummerow

# CONTENTS

# CHAPTER 1

I have learned over the years that when one's mind is made up, this diminishes fear; knowing what must be done does away with fear.
Rosa Parks – 1913-2005

*November 1943, somewhere near Minsk, Russia*

Richard Klausen trudged through knee-deep snow, his feet freezing in the soaked leather boots. Nothing withstood the sub-zero temperatures in the White Russian taiga, certainly not the battered boots and inadequate uniform the Wehrmacht assigned her soldiers.

His trousers stopped mid-calf and had been patched more times than he could count. The steel helmet did nothing to keep the gusty winds from his head, and like most of his comrades he had wrapped an undershirt around his head for better protection.

"Dammit," Richard cursed as he and Karl pushed against the handcart stuck in a snowdrift. Sweat ran down his face and stung his eyes. Moving that cart loaded with materiel was a bitch. They'd been fighting the Russians for two days and this morning Oberstleutnant Schottke had sent the two of them – together with a dozen walking wounded –to the camp for more ammo, more food, more medics, more field dressings, more of everything.

Richard just hoped they would reach the battlefield before their boys ran out of ammunition. It wasn't like last year when he'd been a freshly drafted soldier. Everyone had been bursting with enthusiasm, bagging one victory after another against the Red Army. Supplies had been plentiful and replenishments came on time.

But now? The Wehrmacht was in retreat, one division after another collapsing under the attack of two different, but equally deadly enemies: the Red Army, outnumbering the Germans at least ten to one, and the brutal Russian winter.

With materiel stuck God knows where, a soldier counted himself lucky to own a pair of fitting leather boots without holes. The last functioning truck of their division awaited a delivery of fuel to be set in motion again.

"Push on three!" Karl said and together they shoved against the handcart. It gave a groan and a squeak, and finally crept through the snowdrift.

"Well done, mate," Richard said and fell in pace beside his friend, hauling the handcart between them.

"If we keep up that speed, we'll never reach our boys..."

Karl rubbed his scruffy face with his free hand. Most of the men had given up on the luxury of shaving. Combat and vanity didn't go hand in hand. Besides, a beard yielded some protection from the whipping cold.

"Don't say that. We're making good progress. I can already hear them," Richard said.

As if to prove him right, the sound of MG42 fire cut through the air and in the ensuing moment of silence, they heard the barked instructions of their commanding officer, Oberstleutnant Schottke. Karl and Richard pushed the handcart harder, intent on bringing their comrades the much-needed relief. A distinctive howling sound cut through the air.

"*Stalinorgel*," Richard shouted and dove for cover. The Katyusha rocket launcher was nicknamed Stalin's organ, because the launch array resembled a church organ. But its bone-chilling wheezing sound was the worst nightmare of every German soldier. One of the deadliest Russian weapons, Stalin's organ could fire several dozen rockets within a few seconds.

The fury of the fighting continued unabated – shouting, smashing, screaming, only interrupted by a cacophony of gunfire or mortar fire, and several minutes later the next salvo of Katyusha rockets. To leave cover meant certain injury or death.

Time slowed to a crawl as Richard and Karl lay motionless in a ditch, the cold seeping into their bones, freezing through their clothes and trying to coax the life from their bodies.

Richard clenched his fists at his helplessness. The fumes from the munitions hung in a dense layer above the ground and forced their way down Richard's nostrils and throat, leaving him gasping for breath until he was sure the toxin would suffocate him. A stray rocket hit the handcart; another one blew up a tree less than twenty feet away. The wind lashed and howled mournfully as the fiery assault charred and blackened the earth.

When twilight settled over the taiga, the fighting finally stopped. Richard crawled out of the ditch to witness an overwhelming sight: his battalion had been obliterated, perishing in the carnage. The few surviving comrades were being frogmarched away with their hands behind their heads.

"Everyone gone," Richard said in a faltering voice as he crawled back into the ditch.

Karl only opened his eyes wide and nodded. Silence ensued as both of them contemplated the implications of their thoughts. The relief to be alive mixed with guilt and self-doubt. *If we had pushed harder, arrived earlier...* Logic told Richard that a few more weapons and ammunition wouldn't have made a difference, would have only prolonged the fight against a superior enemy, but his heart wanted to argue.

After a while Karl cleared his throat, saying, "*Knochensammlung.*" Bone collection, as they called the task of searching for wounded comrades.

"Indeed," Richard answered and labored to get up from the frozen ground. They walked the battlefield back and forth, but Ivan had done a good job and left only lifeless bodies scattered about the place. Snow began to fall like a blanket of shame covering the devastation.

An agonizing cry of pain ripped through the still iciness

of the cold winter air. Richard and Karl bolted in the direction of the sound, finding a fellow prone on the icy tundra, nothing more than a mess of blood with limbs missing.

Richard had been in combat long enough to know that the specter of death knocked at the man's door. He couldn't do anything other than caress the man's cheek and wait. He sat down beside the fellow and started talking, telling stories about better times, plentiful food, warm clothes, and beautiful girls. The wounded man's breath rattled and… stopped. Richard stood up, shaking a fist into the sky.

Dark gray clouds jumbled together in one great, frenzied muddle, with no other imaginable purpose but to block out any light and warmth from the pale sun low on the horizon.

"Nothing left for us to do here. Let's go," Richard said and grabbed Karl's hand, needing the comfort of another human soul.

Without a word, they trudged back to the camp to report the annihilation of their battalion. But when they reached the campsite, nothing remained but an empty shell. The battalion's camp had been razed to the ground.

Richard fell to the icy ground, sobs shaking his thin body. He'd been conscripted into this god-awful war the day he'd turned seventeen. His mother's face came to his mind. She'd tried to hide her tears when saying good-bye to her only son, sending him to serve in Hitler's Wehrmacht.

His three sisters Ursula, Anna, and Lotte had put on a brave face, but they couldn't fool him. Lotte, only one year younger than him, had punched him and threatened, "You'd better stay alive, or I'll personally make sure you'll regret dying for the rest of your afterlife."

The image of his fiery, outspoken sister made him smile.

Getting on her bad side wasn't something anyone wanted to experience, so he'd better make sure he survived this mess.

"We need to leave," Richard said.

"But where to?" Karl sat on the ground with sagging shoulders, his head moving back and forth.

"I don't know. Westward. We need to find another division and join up with them." Richard said, his uniform flecked with the debris of battle.

"Hmmm..." Karl glanced over to Richard. "Hmmm..."

The time immediately after a battle was always the worst. The sense of loss and depression could throw a soldier for a loop. Richard couldn't let his friend wallow in his foul mood.

"Get up, numbskull, we have work to do!"

Karl's eyes glinted at the insult and he raised a fist. "Do we? And since when are you the boss here, asshole?"

"Since you're drowning in self-pity. Get your arse up and help me look for food," Richard yelled at his friend, who showed a shadow of a grin before getting up.

"Food. Now we're talking."

Together they scoured what used to be the camp, and found plenty of food scattered about where the field kitchen had been.

They wolfed down bread, dried meat, and boiled potatoes in amounts they hadn't eaten in months, and filled their satchels with all the food they could carry. Then they scrounged around for anything else they could use: weapons, reserve magazines, and warm clothing.

"We have to do what we must," Karl said and pulled off a heavy overcoat and woolen socks from one of the corpses. Richard mirrored his actions, shutting out all thoughts of piety. The fallen comrades had no more use for earthly warmth. But he and Karl would not survive the night in the ragtag clothing draped from their bodies.

Clad each in three pairs of socks and two thick overcoats, Karl and Richard huddled in a ditch, praying to survive the night. They would start their trek into the unknown with the rising sun.

Richard had never wanted to be a soldier. Back at home in Berlin, he'd spent his leisure time with his nose buried in a book. Any book. Much to the dismay of his sister Lotte, who always challenged him to commit one or the other sort of mischief with her. Not entirely unselfishly, he remembered, because in case they were caught, Richard, the boy and the older child, would usually receive the punishment.

In the Hitler Youth, Richard had been content with his place at the end of the line: the small, shy, and gentle boy, unable – or rather unwilling – to keep up with the rest. And if this war hadn't happened, he would have finished school and gotten a degree in teaching in secondary schools. Literature. German language. Instilling his love for the written word in others.

But fate handed him a Wehrmacht uniform and frostbitten toes.

Nothing more than an inept schoolboy, and they'd thrown him into combat. The three weeks' training hadn't really made a difference. Just enough to handle an MP40, the standard infantry weapon, and an MG42 with confidence.

He and Karl had been the youngest in their battalion when they arrived. Seventeen-year-old boys, as opposed to the battle-hardened older and more experienced men.

All gone now.

Eighteen months in brutal combat on the Eastern Front had apparently transformed him into a man.

A survivor.

* * *

Since they didn't have orders and were cut off from their chain of command, they decided to walk until they found a railway track and follow it westward in the hope of encountering another German unit. They sure as hell didn't want to fall into Russian hands.

After many days of mindless walking at day, and huddling in ditches at night, they found a track. Richard and Karl walked several more hours before they heard a hissing and huffing freight train approach. Unsure whether it was a German or a Russian train, they sought cover behind a hedge.

"It's showing the swastika," Karl yelled over the noise and jumped up waving his hands. But the long train didn't slow down.

"Run!" Richard shouted and took off toward the moving train, until he managed to get ahold of the handle bar of one of the last wagons. Karl jumped right up with him and they caught their breath on the tiny platform between two wagons.

"Now what?" Karl asked.

"We need to get inside or we'll soon drop off with frostbitten hands."

After some work they managed to squeeze open the door in a haphazard manner and finally fell on the wooden floor boards of the dirty old train that had no doubt unloaded its supplies somewhere at the front and now returned for more. They both passed out from sheer exhaustion, the monotonous rumble lulling them into sleep.

When they awoke, the day had dawned and threw its meager light on an unknown yet familiar world.

"Any idea where we are?" Richard asked, as they passed once picturesque towns and villages that were now a pitiful picture of devastation.

"Nah...but at least it's warmer," Karl answered, peeling off one of his greatcoats. A heavy sleet fell, dousing everything with gloomy-looking grime.

"We've been driving for how long? Ten hours? Twelve hours?" Their watches had many months ago stopped functioning. If it was the brutal cold in the White Russian taiga, the artillery smoke, or the constant mistreatment, Richard didn't know. Nor did he care.

"Twelve hours westward, which should bring us to somewhere in Poland," Karl said and pointed at the rising sun haloing the sky in their wake. The rays of weak winter sun cast the rubble strewn along the railway into a dim light. Roads and bridges had ceased to exist. Devastation loomed over every horizon. But life went on. Children played about the ruins, not minding the cold and damp.

Richard took the last piece of dried meat from his pack and gulped it down with melted snow from his water bottle. The engine chugged along dragging its load seemingly forever, winding its way around hills and groaning down steep passes. It clanked and wheezed with overwork and lack of steady maintenance, keeping the voracious war machine moving.

"One day this will end, and things will be put right again," Karl said almost to himself. When he got no response from his friend, he asked, "Don't you think so, Richard? This will be over soon?"

"Over for whom?" Richard replied, shrugging his shoulders still warmly encased in the huge gray overcoat. For the first time in weeks he wasn't freezing, but he couldn't summon anything else to feel optimistic about. It was better not to delve into an uncertain future. Instead, he took out a notebook and a pencil he always kept in his breast pocket and wrote a letter home.

It was his way to cope with loneliness and desolation. Writing letters eased his mind off the grimy reality, and let him escape into a better world, at least for a while. None of these letters ever got sent home, because he didn't believe them adequate to express his genuine thoughts. Still, he felt the connection with those he loved while writing and rereading them.

*Beloved Mutter, my dearest sisters,* he wrote, and the unsteady movement of the train gave his words a childish scrawl.

*You will be happy to know that I am well and am traveling with my friend Karl to our next mission. The winter is uncommonly cold for this time of the year with Siberian temperatures of 20 degrees Celsius below zero, strong winds, and four to five feet or more of snow.*

Lots of snow. He remembered the blood on the snow.

Lots of blood. Though he failed to recall many of the details of that fateful day, the sight of blood and the foul stench of carnage remained burned into his brain.

*Don't worry, dearest Mutter, I received a new greatcoat and*

*woolen socks to keep me warm. The food is nothing compared to*
*your wonderful cooking, but at least we don't go hungry.*

Writing the letter didn't help to easy his mind today. His stomach clenched at the reminder of ravaging the supplies meant for an entire battalion.

*Love always,*
*Your son Richard.*

He closed the notebook with a deep sigh.

Karl glanced up saying, "I don't understand why you write all those letters and never post them."

"I don't understand it myself. I…I want to feel close to my family, but I don't want to drag them into this insane war…"

# CHAPTER 2

After twenty-four hours of traveling across the snowbound, war-torn country, the train stopped in Warsaw. A bedraggled Richard and Karl hopped off and asked for directions to the Wehrmacht headquarters, where they reported to the officer in charge.

Leutnant Meisinger cross-referenced his lists with their dog tags three times and still couldn't believe the two filthy, sooty, and exhausted soldiers in front of him belonged to Oberstleutnant Schotte's annihilated battalion.

Reports of the incident had been sketchy since the lost battle against the Red Army and the destruction of camp and communications.

"We'll talk about this tomorrow," he said with a glance at his watch and ordered them to be taken away.

Richard hadn't expected a decoration, but he hadn't expected either that nobody would believe their story. He and Karl were separated, and led away.

"Thanks," Richard said when the soldier opened the door to his room.

"Don't thank me yet," the other man answered and held up the key in his hand before a flush of shame appeared on his face and he looked away.

Richard heard the key turn in the lock and footsteps walking away. *So, I'm a prisoner now? A prisoner of my own army?*

For the moment, though, he didn't care; he entered the bathroom to take a long, lukewarm shower. It was almost like paradise to be clean again. He shaved his matted blond beard and grinned at the mirror. At long last he looked like himself again.

On his return to the room he found a clean Wehrmacht uniform lying on the bunk and a steaming hot meal sitting on the table. At least they were treating him like a soldier and not like the prisoner he effectively was.

Putting on fresh underwear, he sat down to eat every last morsel of his first hot meal in more than two weeks, and then dropped face down onto the bed, passing out within seconds.

Weak sunlight was streaming through the barred window when a knock on the door woke him up. An unknown soldier stepped into the room. "Get dressed and come with me."

Judging by the expression on the man's face, Richard took his cue and dressed in a hurry, swallowing down his questions.

"Follow me."

Minutes later, Richard arrived in an interrogation room.

He hadn't seen Karl since the day before, and wondered if he'd received the same treatment.

"Heil Hitler," Leutnant Meisinger greeted him.

Richard stood at attention and responded with the same greeting.

"I will need a full report of the events. Sit," Meisinger said, and pointed to a table in the middle of the room.

Richard recounted the events of the fateful battle, his voice close to faltering as the memories assailed him.

"Why weren't you with your battalion?" Meisinger asked again and Richard had difficulties suppressing a scream of annoyance. He bit down the snide remark and answered, "As I said before, Karl Wegener and I had been assigned to push the handcart with the reserve ammu–"

"The Wehrmacht has motorized vehicles for that! Why didn't you use them?" Meisinger shouted at him. *You rear-echelon motherfucker, you obviously have never been at the front or you wouldn't talk such bullshit.*

"Leutnant, with all due respect, but–"

"Respect is what I'm missing here." Meisinger shoved himself up and paced behind Richard, whose neck hair stood on end. Having the enemy behind one's back was the last thing any soldier wanted. Although the Leutnant technically wasn't the enemy, it felt like he'd deliberately made himself an adversary without cause.

"Sir," Richard tried again, "all our vehicles were out of fuel. The little we had left was reserved for the sole functioning Panzer–"

"Now you're telling me that your superiors were negligent fools who forgot to order enough materiel? I will tell you something, Soldat Klausen." Meisinger walked around

Richard and stabbed a finger at his chest. "You're telling me a bunch of lies."

"No, Sir, I–"

"The truth!" the Leutnant shouted with a tomato-red face, slamming his fist down on the desk. "I want the truth, Soldat Klausen!"

"Sir, I am telling you the truth," Richard answered as fear gripped him.

"The truth is you are a spy!" The man adjusted his glasses and stared the boy in the face.

"No, Sir, I am not a spy," Richard protested. "I am a loyal soldier and a patriot."

"Your battalion was defeated, the camp ambushed and razed to the ground, and it's just the two of you left to tell the tale?" Meisinger sneered. "Let's have the real story now; I warn you my patience is at an end."

Another officer walked into the room and said with a nod toward Richard, "Has he confessed?"

Richard glanced at the man's epaulettes and recognized him as a major. But despite being several ranks above Leutnant Meisinger, he didn't seem to be interested in taking over the interrogation. Instead he pulled out his Walther P38, loading and reloading it while he stared at Richard.

"There's nothing to confess, Major." Richard's teeth began to chatter.

"At least you haven't forgotten the chain of command," the Major said and weighed the loaded pistol in his right hand. "Major Dietrich it is. And I'm not known for patience. So please spare me the lies and lay the facts on the table."

"We'd been fighting Ivan, I'm sorry, the Red Army, for close to forty-eight hours and were running low on everything. Our battalion leader Oberstleutnant Schotte ordered Soldat Wegener and me to return to the camp and fetch reserves. But that blo…I mean, the handcart got stuck time and again in snowdrifts and the journey took us several hours. Just when we were about to make contact with Oberstleutnant Schotte, we heard a Stalin's organ and dove for cover."

Major Dietrich pursed his lips with disgust. "*Stalinorgel* you say? How many?"

"I don't know. Given how much they fired and how long it takes to reload them, I estimate at least three." Richard folded his hands to keep them from trembling. "The rocket fire lasted several hours. When I crawled out of the ditch we saw a handful of our comrades frogmarched away by the Russians."

"And these Russian troops, who killed everyone else, left you and your little friend alive?" Major Dietrich jumped up, the loaded Walter P38 in hand. "Do you think I'm stupid, Soldat?"

Cold sweat ran down Richard's forehead, but he didn't dare move to swipe it away. "No, Major, of course not. We got lucky, hiding far enough away, or maybe it was the darkness setting in that kept the Russians from doing a thorough search."

"Let me tell you what really happened," Major Dietrich said with a smug grin, "Ivan found you and your little friend, but instead of killing you they offered you a deal. Your life in exchange for becoming a spy for them."

Richard heard the dull clicks of Major Dietrich's pistol, and stars appeared before his eyes as he almost passed out.

To be accused of being a defector meant facing a firing squad.

"No, Major. I didn't. I've been a loyal soldier to the Reich for one and a half years. I wouldn't...those Russian bastards...you really believe I could make common cause with them after they slaughtered all our boys?" Richard asked. For a moment he wished he had died in battle rather than face an interrogator who accused him of such abominable things.

"Well, Soldat Wegener tells a different story." Leutnant Meisinger drew so close, Richard could feel his warm breath on his face.

"I have told you the truth," Richard insisted and wondered if it was true that Karl had admitted to a lie out of fear, or if this was a mere tactic used to break him.

"We have ways to make you tell us the truth." Meisinger barked a laugh and so did the gun-clicking major. They stood up and walked out barking orders to the duty officer to lock Richard up in one of the cells until further notice.

Days and nights passed. Richard lost all hope of ever leaving the lock-up again, his only consolation being that the cell was dry and warm, and he received two meals a day like clockwork.

On the fifth day he was way past caring what happened to him. Scribbling endless letters home, he ran out of blank pages in his notebook and began formulating the sentences in his mind. This, and reciting the grand literature he'd read as a boy helped him keep his sanity.

Many years ago at school, the teacher had made them memorize *The Song of the Bell* by Friedrich Schiller.

Richard's memory was a bit rusty, but the more he recited, the better he remembered. Pacing the cell in the rhythm of the verses, he exclaimed:

*Festgemauert in der Erden*
  *Steht die Form aus Lehm gebrannt.*
  *Heute muss die Glocke werden,*
  *frisch, Gesellen, seid zur Hand!*
*Von der Stirne heiß*
*rinnen muss der Schweiß,*
*soll das Werk den Meister loben;*
*doch der Segen kommt von oben.*

*Zum Werke, das wir ernst bereiten,*
  *geziemt sich wohl ein ernstes Wort;*
  *wenn gute Reden sie begleiten,*
  *dann fließt die Arbeit munter fort.*

*So lasst uns jetzt mit Fleiß betrachten,*
  *was durch schwache Kraft entspringt;*
  *den schlechten Mann muss man verachten,*
  *der nie bedacht, was er vollbringt.*

*Das ist's ja, was den Menschen zieret,*
  *und dazu ward ihm der Verstand,*
  *dass er im innern Herzen spüret,*
  *was er erschaffen mit seiner Hand.*

On the seventh day, the door opened, and a pale Karl stood in front of him. Richard almost cried with joy when he fell into his friend's arms.

"Follow me," an unknown voice said, and Richard's head snapped up to see another soldier standing in the doorframe. Without a word, he and Karl followed him through long halls until he stopped in front of a door and knocked. "Major Dietrich wants to see you now."

Richard's heart pounded in his throat and he clenched his hands into nervous fists.

"Ah, there you are," the major said, looking up from his papers as if he was meeting them for the first time, "Write down your observations in a detailed report, and hand it in to the duty officer. He'll assign you quarters. Stay put until you get new marching orders. Dismissed."

"Yes, Sir, thank you." Richard couldn't believe his good fortune and bolted out of the room, before the major changed his mind and sent him to a gory end by firing squad.

The next two weeks passed in a blur. After long months in grueling combat, it was almost surreal to have so much time on their hands. Karl and Richard spent their days getting to know the Polish capital, attending performances for the troops, drinking plenty of beer and cherishing life to the fullest. It was like the vacation long yearned for, and Richard's only complaint was that he hadn't received furlough to visit his family. But at least he had been able to write a letter to his mother and post it via the army postal service.

Of course the letter had been carefully fabricated and embellished to pass the censors and put Mutter's worries at ease. It made no sense to tell her about his ordeal at the front or in the lock-up.

Karl and Richard were sitting over a beer and a round of skat with another soldier when the door to their quarters opened and the duty officer walked in. They quickly stood to attention, unsure what the officer wanted.

"Klausen and Wegener? Here are your new marching orders. Pack your stuff and report at the gate in thirty," the officer said, handing them papers and slipping from the room again.

Bursting with curiosity, they scanned the documents. Both of them were to join a security division operating out of Lodz, a city about a hundred miles southwest of Warsaw. The main tasks of their new division were anti-partisan duties and surveillance of the Jewish Ghetto.

"I wonder if we're being set up to see whether we are spies or not," Karl said, his voice laced with fear.

"Let's not think the worst. As long as we are true to ourselves, we have nothing to fear." Richard looked forward to the fresh start and intended to make the best of the situation. "Anything's better than going back to the front."

# CHAPTER 3

Upon their arrival in Lodz, they were welcomed by their company leader Leutnant Scherer, who ordered Obergefreiter Hauser to take them under his wing and teach them the ropes of their new assignment.

"We've heard many things about you two," Hauser said, sizing them up with a serious expression on his face. A short military haircut framed his large brown eyes.

"Don't believe everything you hear, Obergefreiter," Richard said and much to his surprise the other man smiled and extended his hand.

"Well then. I'm Johann."

He gave them a tour around the barracks, showed them their bunks in the soldiers' quarters, and explained the nature of their work. "You'll get a better understanding tomorrow when we march out, but basically our job is to scout the activities of the Polish Home Army. Those bloody partisans have been a true pain in the ass, blowing up railway tracks, ammunition dumps, and factories."

Richard had heard about the nuisance the Polish resistance posed, but he'd never given much thought to it. After a few days with his new company, though, things began to fall into place. The halting replenishment at the front, the tardiness and unreliability of the trains, the lack of fuel for the tanks. At least some of this was due to the Home Army blowing up the means of transport and the things to be transported.

Capturing them and stopping their nefarious deeds would give the soldiers at the front a much better chance at survival. He'd long ago stopped thinking that Germany could win this war, but then, what choice did he have but to follow orders? So he'd basically stopped thinking at all. Asking questions wasn't a trait particularly sought after in a simple soldier.

Day after day they formed groups of ten to search the ruins and scour the nearby forests for enemy movement. The Siberian cold had swept across Poland by December 1943, and every night Richard was grateful to bunk down in the barracks instead of having to camp in a makeshift tent.

The comparatively light work, plus the regular and abundant meals they now enjoyed, improved their health immensely. Both Karl and Richard put on at least twenty pounds. Flesh began to cover the bones on Richard's gaunt body and his muscles started to develop. He noticed his uniform had become short at the legs and arms, and strained the buttons of his smart coat.

In a permanent base like Lodz, life was different from the always-moving frontline. For one, army postal service delivered mail like clockwork every week. The men gathered in the courtyard, hooting and hollering when the large canvas mail sacks arrived, eagerly waiting to see if their name would be called and they'd be handed an envelope or a parcel with goodies from home.

Those letters to and from home were a lifeline for them. It didn't matter if letters were late by months or the censors had blacked out portions of the writing. A letter was a treasured possession. Words written with love on a sheet of paper, which mostly brought joy, sometimes sadness or disturbing news. But none of the soldiers would have missed the handout time for anything.

Richard sighed. Again, his name hadn't been called.

Johann strolled over with a parcel in hand and nodded at Richard. "Chin up, boy. The mail can take months to arrive here."

"I know. But still..." Richard turned to walk away.

"Come on. Wanna help me unpack mine?" the older man offered, and Richard's eyes lit up. Together, they unwrapped the parcel and dug out a forearm-sized piece of hard, cured sausage, cigarettes, and knitted socks. Johann pocketed the letter, obviously not willing to share its contents.

"This from your girl?"

"Wish it was." Johann's brown eyes were cast over with sadness as he added, "I've been in this war for five years. On my first furlough, she said she couldn't stand the uncertainty. Didn't want to wait for someone who might never come back." Johann brusquely stood and walked away.

Richard empathized with him, but didn't dare go after the much older, more experienced man. What wisdom did he, an eighteen-year old boy, have to offer? Instead he sought out Karl.

"Hey, Rich, look at this!" Karl waved a sheet of paper at

his friend. "Letter from my mother. She's jazzed. Asking if it's true that I'm still alive. They told her about our battalion and that I'm missing in action. Of course, she assumed the worst."

That piece of information didn't calm Richard's worries. His mother must have received the same note. What if his letter still hadn't reached her and she was living with the burden of losing her only son?

"What about you? Anything?" Karl interrupted Richard's thoughts.

"Nothing. I guess the mail takes a while." Richard turned to hide the tears welling in his eyes. He missed his mother. She had been the backbone of the family, attending to her husband and keeping the four children in line. And he missed his father, who'd been drafted long before Richard. Last thing they heard was that he was prisoner of war in Russia, and no one knew where.

Mutter had gone from pillar to post trying to find out the whereabouts of her husband, to no avail. Richard knew about international conventions regarding the custody of prisoners of war, but he also knew that a Soviet soldier in German captivity couldn't hope for compliance with the Geneva Convention. In his heart he knew that the other side wasn't any better, and that made him worry about his father.

"...is getting married," Karl said, and Richard turned to stare at him. "Who?"

"My sister. Have you even listened to one word I said?" Karl elbowed his friend.

"Sorry. No." Nostalgia swept over Richard. "I...will you ask for a furlough?"

"As if that would make sense. Remember they denied us leave, even though we had no assignment?"

"Hmm."

"Hey, what do you think your sisters are doing?" Karl asked, knowing he could always cheer up his friend by asking about his sisters.

"Ursula got married to her sweetheart almost a year ago. They didn't even give him a furlough for his own wedding. But I guess he got home later this year, and she would be with child by now. She always wanted to be a mother. And Anna, she's working as a nurse." He gave a curt laugh. "I guess that's a very in-demand job right now. "

Karl nodded. "News from Berlin isn't good."

"At least Lotte is with our Aunt Lydia in the country. She's better off there. Less strafing."

"There's only one thing that frightens me more than the *Stalinorgel,* and that's the strafing from the air. You can't outrun an aircraft."

Both fell into silence, each one conjuring up images of their loved ones in better times.

* * *

Christmas arrived to brighten everyone's spirits and the day was celebrated with much enjoyment at the barracks. The girls who worked for the Wehrmacht, the *Wehrmacht-shelferinnen,* and German women living in Lodz had worked many days to prepare a feast for everyone.

Richard barely recognized the barracks: everyone had scrubbed, cleaned, and decorated the quarters with fir sprigs. Every last soldier looked dashing in his clean uniform and polished boots, freshly shaven, and with a new haircut. Richard himself sported a modern cut for his blond hair, and had splurged to go to the barbershop as well.

A joyful tension spread amongst the men and women, as they waited in front of the closed doors to the canteen, where the special dinner would be served.

When the doors opened Richard gasped. The usually bare and practical canteen featured a huge Christmas tree in one corner, sparkling with tinsel. Banners with swastikas hung from the ceiling and the tables were set with white tablecloths, red candles, and green fir sprigs. White ceramic dinnerware replaced the usual metal crockery and a half-liter beer mug adorned every setting.

Richard sat beside Karl and another man from his team, while Johann faced him on the opposite side of the long table. Despite the shortages, the cook and his helpers had outdone themselves by making roast pork and potato salad in quantities that satisfied even the most hoggish man.

The base commander orated with the typical rallying call to victoriously end this war and bring German supremacy to the world. But despite dutifully listening, none of his subalterns were interested in politics or war today.

The mingling smells of roast pork, candle wax, and fir tree made everybody giddy with appetite and nostalgia. As soon as the commander ended his speech, the men and women dug into their meals, joking and giggling. For one day, they would forget the realities of war.

Richard emptied his beer mug and asked for a refill, when Johann stood and put a bottle onto the table. "No more beer. This stuff is killer-diller." He generously poured vodka into the glasses of his comrades.

"*Prost!*" everyone shouted and clinked glasses.

By the time Christmas *stollen* was served for dessert, Richard had difficulties balancing the cake on his fork until it reached his mouth. He barely noticed when one of the *Blitzmädel*, as they nicknamed the girls working for the Wehrmacht, took a seat at the piano and played *O Tannenbaum*.

One after another, the men joined her and belted out traditional Christmas songs at the top of their lungs until the mess hall vibrated with their enthusiastic renderings. Gifts were distributed: greeting cards, warm clothing, tobacco, and eatables, all sent by generous citizens at home for the troops.

Richard appreciated how fortunate he was to be at the barracks. In a moment of nostalgia, he caught Karl's eye and knew that his friend too, was thinking of their last Christmas – spent with their late comrades in an icy, sodden trench.

"Come on, men, drink up!" Johann poured more vodka into his friends' glasses.

"Enough, enough, comrade. I can barely stand," Richard protested but to no avail. Johann insisted they share another drink. And another. Sometime later, Karl passed out.

"Don't expect a boy to do a man's job," Johann snickered, glancing at Karl sprawled out in an awkward position across his chair.

"He is young, barely eighteen," Richard said by way of an excuse for his pal, who would have all manner of painful regrets in the morning.

"What about you, Richard?" Johann teased, "Are you old enough to do a man's job?"

"I believe I am," Richard replied in a drunken slur. "At least I hope I am."

"We'll see about that. Let's go."

"Where are we going?" Richard asked while two of his mates hauled him out of his chair. The floor buckled beneath his feet and he had to lean on his comrades for support.

"Come on, it's a special surprise I have for you." Johann led the way. Dragged along by the two mates, Richard reached a truck full of other drunken soldiers singing and shouting and eager to move on.

"I need to go to bed," Richard protested, and his comrades hooted, "That's exactly where we're taking you."

"That's good," he murmured, focused on keeping the insides of his bowels where they belonged. The raucous merriment in the vehicle became deafening, as drunken men cheered on the equally drunken driver, who careened and screeched at top speed over the bumpy roads until he stopped in the center of Lodz.

Nothing made sense anymore. "Where's my bed?" Richard slurred, as the others bolted out of the truck, producing an ear-splitting roar that ripped through the night and informed the ladies of the brothel that their customers were ready for business.

"Come on, the fun is about to begin." Johann pulled him down from the truck and dragged him along. "Hurry up, man! Or there'll be none of the ladies left for us."

"Ladies?" Richard's eyes widened as understanding hit him.

"Yes, ladies. When was the last time you had sex? I bet it's been much too long." Johann laughed.

"Me?" Richard slumped onto a step and the world started spinning around him.

"Holy shit. It's your first."

It was true, but Richard shook his head. "You go ahead. I just need a minute to clear my head."

Johann didn't waste any time and dashed off. Moments later Richard vomited on his shoes. He managed to stagger back to the base and by the time he arrived most of the alcohol had cleared from his system.

*I'm a complete loser. I can't even sleep with a woman.*

# CHAPTER 4

L odz, February 1944

"This is unacceptable!" Leutnant Scherer yelled at his men. Richard stared at his boots in the hopes the Leutnant wouldn't notice him.

"Obergefreiter Hauser, step forward."

Everyone in the room except Johann, who stepped forward to receive the brunt of the tirade for his team, sagged with relief. As if the bitter cold weather wasn't enough to deal with, the pesky Polish Home Army had increased their sabotage activities with the New Year.

The hostile elements of nature should have slowed them down. It certainly reduced the vigilance of Richard and his team, who spent as little time outside as possible. But those Polacks seemed to run on nothing but vodka, and everyone knew that booze only tasted better the colder it got.

"The bloody partisans blow up the bridge on the main North-South train connection and all I get from you lightweights is a shrug?" As he yelled at Johann, the Leutnant's face turned a vibrant shade of crimson red.

"Leutnant, we have been making daily rounds—"

"Shut up with that nonsense. I want results, not excuses."

"Yes, Leutnant." Johann presented the perfect picture of misery, and once again Richard was glad he was only a simple soldier executing orders.

"In the last two weeks, the partisans blew up two railroad bridges and one tunnel. They cut communication lines, bombed fuel depots, and attacked pockets of our soldiers. This issue is more than a problem; it is an embarrassment for the entire base! I have been raked over the coals by high command, demanding I pull up my socks or else…" Leutnant Scherer snapped for air, and blood vessels on his forehead and neck popped out.

His heated stare seared into every man present, before he pointed a finger at Johann and growled, "You will fix this. Now. Double up your efforts and don't return to base without the head of a partisan."

"Yes, Leutnant," Johann said. "Perhaps more men may be assigned to the scouting team, as half of my men are on sick leave with frostbite. The weather has limited our mobility—"

"It hasn't limited the mobility of those devils, Hauser!" Wild with rage, Leutnant Scherer flailed his arms through the air until he pointed a shaking finger at Johann's chest. "I have no men to spare. Make do with what you have. Have those lazybones return from the infirmary. Mobilize your informants. Bring me good news within forty-eight hours or you'll all be sent to the front. Dismissed."

The Leutnant left and a murmuring went through the room.

"The commander spoke of informants," Richard said. "Do we have such people we can count on?"

"We don't," someone replied. "No one except for the prostitutes talks to us these days."

"And with the ladies you must watch your mouth, because they're usually spies for the partisans," Johann said. "But enough of that, you've heard the Leutnant. Who wants to serve at the front?"

Nobody raised their hands.

Except for Richard and Karl none of them had witnessed a battle with the Red Army firsthand, but hearing about it and seeing the maimed and wounded transported home in hospital trains deterred them from volunteering.

Johann drew up a fresh roster and assigned teams of two to scout around for any information that would help their mission. Richard groaned when he was teamed up with Holger, a handsome man in his mid-twenties with blond hair and blue eyes like Richard himself. He hated Holger's womanizing ways and his constant bragging about his newest conquest.

"Ah, boy. A few hours with friends at the bar can tell us all we need to know." Holger smirked and thumped Richard on the back. "Let's have an evening out, meet some of my lady friends, have a laugh and a few drinks. I guarantee it will be worth it. You watch and learn."

Richard doubted the success of Holger's proposition, but since the man topped him in rank, he had the say. Soon the two of them were sitting in the dimly lit tavern, and beautiful young ladies swarmed Holger.

"Come here, doll," Holger said and sat a pretty brunette on his lap. Alcohol flew freely. Lips locked. Hands moved.

Richard nipped on his beer, doing his best to look away. Why had they come here? He sure as hell wasn't interested in dallying with a Polish girl. If he ever had a girlfriend, he wanted her to be a decent woman, one who didn't hang out in bars and jump in the laps of random soldiers. Richard wanted to walk out with her and court her, hold her hand, and get to know her before pressing the first kiss on her lips.

"What's your name, doll?" Holger asked, one hand firmly on the woman's thigh, the other one pouring more vodka into her glass.

"Hannah," she said running her tongue across her lips, before she emptied the glass. "I fancy strong men. Like you." She licked her lips again.

"And I fancy beauties like you." He put his arms around the girl and held her close, whispering in a low voice, so that Richard barely understood, "I promise you a night full of delight and plenty of food to take home to your family, but first I need to know something."

The girl snuggled up to him and her eyes gleamed at the mention of food.

"You wouldn't know where the resistance members are hiding out?" he purred into her ear.

Hannah's back stiffened with the question. "What do you want from them?"

"Talk, only talk," Holger said, showering her face with little kisses. "And there's a lot of food for you. Do you like roast pork?"

Richard could see how the girl fought with herself, but

finally relented. "The village up north, Baluty. You promise nothing will happen to them?"

"I promise, my doll, and now it's time for us to have some fun. Go get your coat," he patted her butt and winked at an astounded Richard. "See how easy that was? Now you return to base and bring Johann the news, I have business to attend to."

Johann was pleased by the intelligence, and Leutnant Scherer was so impressed he arranged to conduct a surprise dawn raid with the reinforcement of an entire SS squad. In the wee hours of the night, the surveillance team set out to search the little village of Baluty for resisters.

## CHAPTER 5

The raid on Baluty reminded Richard of the frontline, except their opponents were civilians and didn't carry weapons. The odds were stacked heavily in their favor this time. In the village, about twenty men jumped off the truck and entered the houses, surprising people in their sleep and hauling every living soul outside, where they lined them up for questioning. Women and children to the left, men to the right.

But no questioning took place.

The SS squad arrived in their slick black uniforms with the red armbands showing the black swastika on white ground. Richard froze with shock when the SS-Scharführer aimed his pistol at the temple of the first man in line and pulled the trigger. The bile crawled up the back of his throat. He'd seen many cruel battles, but never such cold-blooded murder. He cast a silent plea for help toward Johann, who shook his head. An Obergefreiter couldn't pull rank against an SS-Scharführer.

"What are you waiting for? The work doesn't do itself!" The SS-Scharführer yelled at his men, who repeated his actions until no Polish man was left standing and the pristine carpet of white snow was covered in crimson blood. The shrill screams of the womenfolk as they lamented the horror of the morning pierced Richard's ears. He closed his eyes for a moment, unable to stand the sight of such evil.

"Now, let's get to the fun part and show these women what happens to traitors to the German Reich," the SS-Scharführer called out and grabbed the first female within arm's reach. Tearing off her clothes, he raped the poor woman under the hooting and hollering of his squad.

The other women raced away, intent on hiding in their houses, but to no avail. Dozens of SS troopers searched the village and systematically and brutally raped every female they got ahold of.

"We're out of here," Johann ordered his men to retreat while the brutality of their compatriots raged through the village. "There's nothing for us to do when the SS is in charge."

Richard stumbled along the road, bumping against Holger, who spat out angrily, "Get a hold of yourself. Be a man, for God's sake!"

"...but... they killed... murdered... everyone..."

"Those Polacks would kill you in a heartbeat. Do you know how much damage these bastards have done us? How much brave German blood has been shed by these snakes? They deserved it."

Richard shook his head. In his eighteen months at the front he'd never had to question the why. War was war. Soldiers killed soldiers. But killing and raping civilians?

36

"Why do they have to rape the women?" Richard's voice shook under the force of his emotion.

"What of it! They're only Poles, an inferior race. These women should be happy to be done by a real man at least once in their lives. If it wasn't for Johann and his wretched sense of morale, we'd be joining in the fun now." Holger kept complaining as they marched toward the truck.

"Fun?" Richard couldn't believe his own ears.

"You still have to learn a lot, my boy, before you become a man. Besides, it teaches them a lesson, shows them who's the boss here. These women and their men will never question German superiority again." Holger added, "What we both need is a good hot meal."

Richard was about to jump onto the truck when a movement caught his eye. A small person slipped inside a shed at the end of the village. He thought of ignoring it, but several others had seen it as well.

"There's another one!" someone shouted.

Johann seemed to hesitate for a moment but then gave the expected order. "Everyone down and search the area in pairs."

The team dashed in different directions and soon the first soldiers came back with captured villagers. Richard and Holger entered the shed just when a person tried to sneak out and run for the woods. Richard acted swiftly and grabbed the young woman by her long brown hair as she struggled to flee.

Her beautiful brown eyes met his and the expression of fear mixed with fury bolted through his heart. *She is so young and beautiful. Why does she have to be in the wrong place at the wrong time?*

Heavy footsteps thumped inside and one of the SS soldiers grabbed the girl's arm. Richard's heart squeezed knowing she would have to endure the inevitable at the SS trooper's hands and he barked at him, "Back off! I saw her first, she's mine!"

Surprised by Richard's sudden outburst the other man held up his hands and grinned. "Hey, no big deal. Have your fun and I'll take her next."

The frantic girl in Richard's grip kicked, jabbed, punched, and kneed, reckless of where she hit, while Holger and the SS man cheered him on with comical advice. For lack of a better idea, Richard dragged her toward some bales of hay piled up at the back of the shed. She put up more of a fight than some of his comrades would be able to, but Richard slapped her hard across the face and when she stumbled at the impact, he pinned her on the floor.

"Go on, Richard, show the bitch who's the boss," Holger shouted and then waved the SS man away. "Let our baby have some privacy for his first time. We'll come back later and show the bitch how real men do the job."

Richard wanted to cry with joy when he heard the door close behind them, leaving him alone with the beautiful brunette.

Out of the corner of the dirt-covered window he saw the two men take out cigarettes, walking back to the truck, waiting for him to finish his business.

"Stop! Stop struggling!" he hissed. "I'm not going to harm you."

But the girl didn't hear him, so caught up in her own terror was she. She wormed her hand free and ripped her nails into the flesh on his face. Richard grabbed her wrists and pinned them firmly above her head. Her curses mixed with the intermittent sounds of gunshots as a new batch of captives were picked off.

"Please stop struggling," he begged. "I'm not going to hurt you, but those other men will."

Her knee landed in his crotch and she used the moment of pain to wiggle out from under him. Richard grabbed her by the shoulder. "Stop, please." His words came out in gasps, "I could never hurt you...I will help you...calm down...don't make things worse for yourself."

It seemed he finally got through to her and she slumped limply against him.

"Thank you," she whispered in German and gave him a soft smile that moved his heart. "But how?" They didn't have much time to devise a plan.

A pigeon used the quietude to fly across the shed. Richard took his pistol, aimed at the pigeon sitting under the roof, and fired.

It fell silently.

"Lie still," he said, rubbing the pigeon's blood over her and himself. Then he walked toward the exit, just in time to bump into Holger, who'd come running at the sound of the shot.

"You fine?" Holger asked with a glance at his blood-stained, disheveled comrade.

"A real wildcat," Richard said, frowning.

"Did you give it to her?"

"What do you think?" he replied impudently as he made a display of straightening his clothes. "Sorry I ruined the fun for you."

"No worries. There'll be others. Although I do like me a

wildcat." Holger patted him on the back, and nodded toward the truck, where Johann was giving the sign to leave. *Thank God, Johann.*

As he jumped onto the back of the truck, Richard glanced back to the shed where he'd left the beautiful girl with the enticing smile. She reminded him a lot of his sister Lotte, another wildcat. His strong and independent sister never backed down and fought harder than most of the boys, including him. He grinned. Even Lotte wouldn't stand a chance against the battle-hardened version of him anymore. Apart from the muscles formed by daily exercise, he'd also grown at least three inches in the past year and a half – painfully reminded by his toes confined in too small shoes.

He cocked his head. This was the first time in several months that he could think of his favorite sister without his heart squeezing tight. *I hope she's all right. Anna and Ursula too. And Mutter.*

As the engine fired up, they caught a last glimpse of the village. The SS had started torching the houses, and the women and children howled piteously. Richard's last impression, before the truck rounded a corner was one that would haunt him for the rest of his days. Desolate people slumped on the icy ground, beating their faces and bodies with their palms. This incident went beyond war and served no purpose, except to satisfy the cruelty and sadism of a few.

Back in his quarters he found Karl. "This is not war. This is a crime."

"I don't even want to think about it. I thought we'd seen

the ugly side of humanity, but this…?" Karl dashed to the bathroom to vomit.

Richard fell face down onto his bunk, his stomach flipping over in protest. As he dozed off into a sleep plagued with nightmares, the sweet face of the beautiful brunette followed him, her brown eyes full of gratitude. "I hope she's safe," he murmured in his sleep.

# CHAPTER 6

After the raid on Baluty, the partisan activity in the area decreased considerably. Several weeks later Reichsstatthalter Arthur Greiser visited the base. Soldiers gathered in the mess hall, half curious, half nervous at the rather curious event.

"What do you think he wants?" Karl whispered.

"No idea, but I don't think it's bad. Look how Leutnant Scherer beams," Richard said and pointed to the base commandant. The usually grumpy man looked like a child on Christmas Eve, fussing over the mayor.

"Shush," Johann warned them, as Greiser and Scherer stepped onto the wooden platform at the side of the hall.

"It has come to my knowledge that the security unit made an essential discovery that helped us to annihilate the nest of the partisans, who'd been hiding right under our noses. I want to personally thank and congratulate everyone for his part in such an important mission." Greiser paused for a moment before he continued, "but our efforts cannot weaken. Not until the day when our great Führer announces the total victory of Germany over her enemies can we bask in our heroic deeds."

Richard willed the rising bile down his throat. *What exactly is heroic about murdering unarmed civilians?*

"...until that day we must pursue the Total War and extinguish every last Jew from the face of our Earth..." Richard tuned out the rest of Greiser's speech.

"Heil Hitler!" a soldier shouted, and everyone responded with a rousing "Sieg Heil!"

After rewarding everyone involved in the raid on Baluty with an extra day's leave, the Reichsstatthalter and the Base Commander left the mess hall.

"Total War, my ass," someone said.

"I'll bet that fat pig has never gotten a close-up of an enemy soldier," another man answered.

Richard turned around and stared into the eyes of Andreas, a man he especially disliked for his arrogance. "What about you? Have you ever had a damn Mosin-Nagant rifle pointed at your head?"

"Don't get all shitty on me, milksop. Aren't you quivering with fear already?" Andreas responded and gave a girlish scream.

Karl put a hand on Richard's shoulder, meant to calm him down, but it only served to rouse him more. He shook Karl's hand off and closed the distance to Andreas. Richard didn't care that Andreas had at least thirty pounds on him; he stabbed him with his finger. "I'll tell you what. You're a hopeless coward who has balls only for perpetuating violence against women and children. How about you take it up with someone your size for once?"

43

"You mean yourself, milksoppy baby?" Andreas sneered and the next moment Richard's fist landed straight at his chin. In the ensuing tumult, Richard felt several men grab him, pinning him face down on the floor. He didn't care.

"Let me up! Goddamn bastards!" Out of his mind with rage, shame, and guilt he struggled frantically like the girl in Baluty had done, until he heard Johann's voice in his ear. "You stay down until you calm down."

Richard listened to the roaring blood in his ears, surprised at his own outburst. He'd never started a fight before. But for the entire week, he'd been sickened with disgust, bottling up the shame he felt about the hideous and barbaric acts of the SS. He didn't want to be part of this.

After a while, the fight went out of him and his body became limp. "I'm calm now."

Johann ordered the other men to let him up and said, "A word in the office, Richard. I'll deal with you later, Andreas." Johann didn't have his own office, but in his position as team leader he was allowed to use the Feldwebel's for private discussions.

"What's wrong with you, Richard? That kind of behavior can land you in a court-martial."

"I'm sorry. It won't happen again," Richard pressed out through thinned lips.

Johann put a hand on his shoulder. "I've been worried about you for quite a while now. Let me help you. Tell me what's bothering you."

"It's nothing."

"Liar."

"I...am disgusted with myself. Sickened by what's happening. Sickened by what my country has become. The hypocrisy. This is not war anymore, this is a yawning abyss of sadism and inhumanity. I am a soldier, not a cold-blooded killer. I hate this! I can't go on like this!" Richard burst out.

Johann took a moment before he answered. "I agree with you that some unfortunate things are happening. The SS especially doesn't adhere to the morals that used to apply to the Wehrmacht. But this doesn't mean we're all bad. We need to follow our orders, fight for our country, and protect our families."

"Even if this war is disgusting and unjust?"

"Even then. We're soldiers. We follow orders. If we didn't, the whole Reich would crumble under the burden imposed upon her. We may not understand every command, because we don't have the big picture and strategic outlook our leaders have." Richard glimpsed pain in Johann's eyes for a moment. "What would happen to Germany if the Wehrmacht refused to do what is expected of her? Our enemies would overrun us, murder, rape, and loot their way across our Fatherland. We can't let this happen. We need to protect our families."

Richard scoffed. "So we're murdering, raping, and looting first to prevent them from doing the same to us?"

"I don't agree with what the SS is doing, but I have no means of stopping them. Nobody has."

"You're right," Richard said. "You're such a good friend to me. I don't deserve your kindness and patience."

"Bollocks. Now get out here before I change my mind and file a report."

\* \* \*

The sun had gathered strength and melted the snow. At long last the days became longer and warmer, much to everyone's delight. Gone were the days of frostbitten toes and fingers, lost eyelashes or eyelids dropping off like a piece of dead skin.

Richard used his leisure time to sit in the wind-sheltered courtyard, soaking up rays of sunshine, while turning a letter from his mother in his hands. His heart had leapt with joy that morning during mail distribution, but he hadn't mustered the courage to read the letter for fear of bad news.

It was the first sign of life from his family in half a year.

"Still staring at the envelope? Catch!" Karl strolled over and threw him a few walnuts he'd promoted God knows where.

Richard glanced up and caught them with one hand. "Thanks, and yes."

"You're a puzzle, pal. For the past six months you've been whining about the lack of correspondence and now you don't open it?"

"I will...I wanted to find a quiet and peaceful place first."

"Are you crackers? There's not a peaceful place anywhere in Europe from the Ural Mountains to the Atlantic Ocean – not that I know of."

Richard gave his friend a good-natured kick in the shins. "War aside, I was looking for a place without nosy comrades butting into my private affairs."

"And here I thought I could offer to read the letter for you," Karl said with an exaggerated grin.

"Why don't you stick your nose in your own business?"

"Because as you might have noticed if you had paid attention, I didn't receive anything today. And I wouldn't be the first one to read your private letter either." That much was true. And the offer tempted him – somewhat.

"No way. But give me another walnut and I might just read some parts aloud for you."

"Well, if that isn't an offer." Karl grinned and produced two more walnuts from his pockets. "Scoot over. I'm all ears."

Doing his best to hide the slight tremble in his hands, Richard unfolded the paper, black lines of censor's ink blocking out entire sentences, and read, "My dearest boy–"

"You're eighteen and your mother still calls you dearest boy?" Karl teased.

"Shut up if you want to hear."

"Fine, go on."

*You can't imagine how elated I was to receive your letter. The high command had sent me a telegram that you were missing in action near Minsk. Despite your sisters' assurances that this didn't necessarily mean you're dead, I had a hard time coming to terms with your disappearance. Please don't do this to me ever again! I'm much too old for such grievances.*

Richard snorted. "That's typical for Mutter. Does she think I've gone missing on purpose?"

"You could." A wistful expression appeared on Karl's face. There wasn't a single soldier in their former unit who hadn't been attacked by *Frontkoller*, battle fatigue, wanting to leave it all behind.

Usually the man in question soon got over this mood, but not always. They'd had to tackle Hansen to the ground with four men to keep him from taking off. And Bundner snuck out at night, walked five miles westward before the Ivan got him.

Richard continued reading.

*So much has happened.*

*Ursula's husband died last May, but your sister has been holding up very well. Poor girl. She's been a real help with everything, especially now that Anna moved out. Anna is working with the Charité Hospital and they offered her employment housing. I didn't agree with her living on her own, but since the dreadful Englishman is bombing Berlin almost every night, it's probably for the best that she doesn't have to walk home at night.*

Richard's hand holding the letter sunk to his lap. Deep in the East he'd almost forgotten that Germany fought a war on two fronts. Or three…or four…who had time to count the enemies?

*Your Aunt Lydia had a new baby last October, a girl called Rosa. Since this is her sixth child, she'll be decorated with the Second Class Silver Cross this coming May on Mother's Day. If Anna and Ursula can get a few days off, we will all be traveling to Kleindorf. I so wish you could meet us there.*

He needed a few seconds to recall this aunt of his, his mother's youngest sister, who lived in a farm village in Lower Bavaria with her growing flock of children.

*Please take care of yourself and send letters whenever you can.*

*Love*

*Mutter*


"See? No bad news. Aren't you glad I told you to read the letter?" Karl chuckled.

"Hmm…she didn't mention anything about Vater, which means she has no news about him."

"We can only hope Ivan will treat him half-decently."

Karl put a hand on Richard's arm. "He'll do fine. He's a soldier like we are. Strong. Tough."

Richard kicked a pebble with his boot. "She didn't mention Lotte either."

"That's your youngest sister, right? The one who was sent to live with your aunt in the country?"

"Yes," Richard answered and fingered a picture from his pocket. It had been taken a little more than one year ago in January 1943 and showed his three sisters on Ursula's wedding day.

Johann entered the courtyard, obviously seeking a sunny place to relax for a few minutes. When he saw the two of them, he strolled over asking, "Pictures from home? Can I see?"

"Sure." Richard handed him the photograph. "The blonde one in the middle is my oldest sister Ursula on her wedding day. *Stahlhelmtrauung*."

The other men nodded. Marriages by proxy had become the norm between combat soldiers and their sweethearts back home.

"Her husband died before returning home," Richard continued. "The blonde on the left is Anna. She's working as a nurse at the Charité in Berlin. She's the ambitious one of us four, a brilliant A-student. Always wanted to become a scientist, but my parents wouldn't permit it. Then the one on the right with the untamed red curls is Lotte, the youngest. She'll turn eighteen this coming September."

"They're all pretty dolls, but the redhead's a knockout," Johann said appreciatively.

"Don't even think about it! She's my sister."

"No worries, pal. She's much too young for me." Johann grinned and handed the photograph back.

"This terrible war will end soon, and we will all return to our lives and our loved ones again," Karl said.

"Will we? Will they all be there?" Fear gripped Richard, who was still wondering why his mother hadn't mentioned Lotte in the letter.

# CHAPTER 7

Feldwebel Huber gathered all security units in the mess hall.

"The Ghetto in Lodz is the last existing flocking place of Jews in the Reich, and Reichsführer Himmler has called for its final liquidation. Therefore, Reichsstatthalter Greiser asked the Wehrmacht to secure transport for the eighty thousand Jews currently inhabiting the ghetto."

Nobody spoke, but the question hung in the room. *Where will they go?*

"All able-bodied men and women will be resettled to start a new life in the East." Feldwebel Huber assigned tasks to the different units and reminded them that it was of utmost importance to not disappoint the Reichsstatthalter.

A murmur went through the room. Most of the men could care less about that administrative prick and the spiteful SS he commanded.

On the way back to their quarters, Richard took Karl

aside asking, "Resettled to the East? Do you believe that crap?"

"Maybe it's true. We've been in Russia. There's plenty of empty land."

"Empty, devastated and scorched land. And…do you really think the Soviets will welcome hundreds of thousands of Jews from all over Europe into their country?"

Karl shrugged, but the expression on his face clearly indicated that he did *not* believe it. "Maybe another ghetto somewhere? What other possibility is there?"

"Perhaps we prefer not to know."

"You can't be serious, Richard. That's unthinkable. Impossible. Detestable."

Richard didn't pursue the topic further. Some things were best left unsaid. In any case, if someone overheard them, his remarks would be a sure way to find out firsthand the final destination of those transports.

The tension in the barracks increased on a daily basis. The front was crumbling faster than the Wehrmacht could retreat. Paper pushers all over occupied Poland feared for their comfortable positions far behind the frontlines.

Rumors ran amok.

It didn't help that the Polish Home Army were reinvigorated in their acts of sabotage, fueled by the change of season, both in temperature and the advancing Russians. Richard's unit worked longer shifts in a frantic attempt to keep the resistance from damaging supply lines; an attempt at giving their pals at the front a fighting chance against the Red Army. It seemed with every blood-soaked yard of earth they took back from the German occupier, the Russians grew bolder, stronger, more determined, while the

Wehrmacht depleted her materiel: Panzers, machine guns, ammunition, food, clothing, but most of all: men. There simply weren't enough men left in the Reich to replace those falling every day.

Sixteen-year olds were sent into combat to *train on the job*. Richard scoffed. Cannon fodder. The poor boys didn't stand a chance.

Richard walked through the woods on patrol to reconnoiter the villages bordering the base. The trees were bursting with fresh green foliage. He inhaled the sharp and sweetly scented air, thinking how different the countryside looked in spring. In times of peace it must have been a beautiful place to live.

But something else had changed. Something that couldn't be explained by longer days and more sunshine. A different energy hung in the air, competing with the smell of flowers. An energy hidden from the five human senses, but he still picked it up, although it took him a long time to identify it.

Back in one of the villages, his unit was patrolling the street, when someone yelled, "Better you start packing your bags and run, Krauts. Ivan is coming to get you!"

A shiver ran down Richard's spine – the same tension ratcheting up in the army base could be felt outside. But here it was hope. Hope to be liberated from the detested occupier.

Soon.

The image of the beautiful girl from Baluty came to Richard's mind. *I hope she's alive and safe.* Despite logic, he longed to see her again.

Moments later a lump of dirt hit him in the face.

Everyone dropped down on one knee, scrambling his submachine gun at the ready. Karl and Richard, due to year-long habit, were the first ones to aim, but the civilians had melted into their surroundings already. A few of the soldiers fired nervous volleys of bullets into the air.

"Stop shooting," Johann yelled. "They're gone. Keep your guns at the ready and retreat to the truck."

Back at the base another nasty surprise waited for them.

During their patrol two medical officers had arrived in Lodz, and every man considered nonessential in running the base had been ordered to gather in the mess hall for a physical exam. Not surprisingly the vast majority received category 1, fit for service at the front. Marching orders would be given within the next days.

Andreas passed by, wearing a desolate expression that quickly transformed into hostility when he recognized the security unit. "Lucky bastards. You are to stay."

Richard had every right to feel *Schadenfreude* for the arrogant fellow, but he felt only empathy. "Sorry, lad. My advice if you want to survive this hell: Shoot first; think later."

"Babyface, and you know this how?" Andreas broke out into a smirk, but suddenly the cockiness fell from his face and his eyes widened. "You're not going to tell me you've been there?"

"A full eighteen months," Karl said.

"Holy shit," Andreas murmured. "Sorry, I had no idea. You look so...young."

"No problem." Richard grinned. "We'll have a beer when you return. Don't make me wait in vain."

The soldiers in Richard's unit looked at one another,

their tired faces awash with relief. At this point in the war no one was enthusiastic anymore – maybe with the exception of those back home, thousands of miles away from the front who'd never seen a trench filled with the dead, or hospital trains filled with maimed and wounded.

# CHAPTER 8

In the following days a bunch of *Wehrmachtshelferinnen* arrived in Lodz to take over the positions of the men leaving for the front.

Cheerful faces. Happy eyes. Dapper uniforms. The girls were excited about their new jobs. And the boys loved the female company. Of course, romantic involvement and inappropriate advances were strictly forbidden and could land a guy in lock-up, but there were clever ways around it.

"Why don't we invite a few of the *Blitzmädel* on a night out in town?" Holger suggested, using the nickname of the helper girls derived from the distinctive lightning-flash emblem on their uniform.

"But won't that get us in trouble?" Karl asked with burning ears. He'd already had his eye on a petite blonde with a knockout figure.

Johann entered the discussion, "Not if we make it a friendly group event. You know, protecting the girls from the locals. As long as we stay together none of the officers will object. Although," he said with a wink, "I might not be able to count very well after a few beers."

Said and done.

Richard enjoyed the night out in town, even though finding a girl was the furthest thing from his mind, since he was secretly hoping to see the brunette from Baluty again. The memory of the quick moment when she'd relaxed her body against his still sent hot shivers through his veins. He wished, yearned, and dreamed about seeing her again and placing a kiss on her soft skin.

Soon enough the cheerful group of young adults split into pairs, and when curfew arrived, Johann kept his promise and didn't count his boys.

The next morning another new arrival was the topic of conversation in the mess hall.

"Have you heard? A Waffen-SS unit arrived in Lodz," Holger said.

"Waffen-SS? What do they want here? Shouldn't they rather be where the frontline is?" a fellow called Frank answered.

"They're here to oversee closing down the Ghetto and resettling the eighty thousand Jews." Richard glanced around. The voice belonged to Feldwebel Huber.

"Does the mayor think we can't do this?" someone bickered and the Feldwebel cast him a severe look.

"You'll soon be happy that the Dirlewanger brigade is doing the dirty work for you."

A murmur ran through the room. Every last man had heard about SS-Oberführer Oskar Dirlewanger and his men. Originally composed of poachers, common criminals, and concentration camp prisoners, nobody had taken them seriously – at first.

But the Dirlewangers, as they proudly called themselves, had soon taken a stand. A reputation of unparalleled terror preceded them and a trail of sadistic violence and unspeakable atrocities was left in their wake.

Richard's stomach turned queasy at some of the things he'd heard. Under normal circumstances the degenerates would all have been court-martialed out of the Wehrmacht. According to the grapevine the Dirlewangers made up with brutality what they lacked in discipline. Alcohol flowed in abundance and members of the troop or its leader were rarely seen in a sober condition.

"Let's go." Richard elbowed Karl.

"Dirlewanger, my ass," Karl echoed Richard's own thoughts as they walked back to their quarters.

"If they're here to close down the Ghetto, I'm inclined to believe the resettlement is a hoax."

"You can't be sure of that," Karl objected.

"And I don't want to find out. I'm afraid what we've seen in Baluty hasn't been the worst yet."

Karl's face paled. "I don't want to be part of that."

"Me neither."

\* \* \*

An ominous haze hung over the atmosphere during the next days, as if everyone waited, expected even, for something bad to happen. It didn't take long. One evening, news came in that subversives had shot two German officers in the center of town.

The very next morning the retaliation was set into motion. Wehrmacht soldiers patrolled the streets of Lodz, securing the exit roads out of town. The Dirlewangers, drunk and rowdy even in the early morning, set out to break doors and drag men, women, and children out of their houses. The marketplace filled with a crowd of Poles, quivering with fear. Some tried to escape, but after the first shots rang through the air, none of the civilians dared to run.

Richard looked at the miserable faces of those expecting to meet their maker. He turned even as the bile rose in his throat. Some kind of retaliation was appropriate, or the Poles would continue to shoot German officers, but he resented the manhandling and abuse of innocent citizens. Slaughtered bodies littered the ground in the tumult that followed. Richard fisted his hand with rage and helplessness as he witnessed how a Pole bleeding from the head staggered and dropped like a felled tree when another rifle butt struck him. The rampaging SS-trooper stepped over his body and continued his riot elsewhere.

Richard sprinted to the wounded man and bent over him, lifting his head to let him drink from his flask. An outraged scream from behind pierced Richard's ears and when he turned his head he noticed SS-Oberführer Dirlewanger himself screaming at him.

"Shoot that Polish bastard!" Dirlewanger commanded.

Richard's eyes became wide. "I'm not going–"

"Shoot, I say! This is an order!"

Richard knew what happened to soldiers who disobeyed a direct order, but he stood firm. "No. He's unarmed. And wounded."

"Coward!" The furious monster collared Richard and yelled, "Anyone here man enough to do the job?"

Moments later one of his men stepped forward and aimed at the Polish man lying on the street.

*Bang!*

In that tortured moment, Richard made a decision.

Later in the barracks, he was called to Leutnant Scherer's office. He'd committed too serious an offence to let go without consequences.

"Soldat Klausen, you disobeyed a direct order," the Leutnant said with a stern voice.

"I'm sorry, Leutnant. But I cannot murder an innocent civilian."

"I agree with you, but my hands are bound here. Dirlewanger is livid and demands you be punished. So what am I going to do with you?" Leutnant Scherer's face suddenly seemed tired, clueless even.

"Sir…may I make a suggestion?"

"You may."

Richard mustered all his courage to go through with his plan. "I wish to be transferred to a fighting unit."

Leutnant Scherer's jaw dropped to the floor and he ran a hand through his cropped hair before he answered. "Let me get this right. You're asking me for a transfer to the front?"

"Yes, Sir."

"You know this is suicide. Nobody in their right mind volunteers to go to the front. Not when the Russians are kicking the living daylights out of our boys."

"I know this, Leutnant. But I would rather die honorably on the battlefield than be part of the atrocities committed against civilians."

"If this is your wish, I will expedite your marching orders," Leutnant Scherer said and put a heavy hand on Richard's shoulder. "I admire your strength of conviction. You're a good man. Never forget this. Dismissed."

Once he'd left the Leutnant's office, Richard returned to his quarters, berating himself for the stupidity of his decision.

"How'd it go?" Karl, Johann, and the other boys had been sitting on pins and needles.

Richard smirked. "Fairly well, I guess...he transferred me to a fighting unit."

His mates blanched and everyone talked at once, until Johann silenced them and said, "I'll talk to him. He made a rash decision—"

"It was my suggestion."

Heads snapped around. Mouths gaped wide open.

"Your idea?" Karl finally broke the silence.

"Yes. I can't live with myself knowing I am part of these cruelties." Richard flopped onto his bunk and tried a lopsided grin. "I'd rather take my chances on the battlefield. I mean, it's not like I haven't been through that already."

# CHAPTER 9

K arl had decided to request a transfer as well and accompany Richard on the new mission. Their belongings packed, there was nothing left to do but wait for the troop transport destined to replenish the divisions of the *Heeresgruppe Mitte*, the Army Group Center.

Richard fetched paper and pencils and wrote a letter to his mother.

*Dearest Mutter,*

*You may not understand my reasons, but let me assure you I'm not acting in a rash or unconsidered manner. In fact, I have given this decision my utmost thought and I am convinced that I am better suited to defend our country on active duty.*

*It may or may not be possible to communicate from where I go next, but please continue writing, and keep me in your thoughts and prayers. Tell me how you are holding on, how the situation is in Berlin, and how my sisters are.*

*I have the photograph of my sisters on Ursula's wedding day with me at all times. It gives me comfort and brings me near to my family. May I please ask you to send me a picture of yourself as well?*

*Your loving son,*
*Richard.*

He'd just folded the letter and carefully slid the photograph into his breast pocket when Johann came into the quarters.

"You're leaving," Johann said, stalling.

"Yes, I am. Thank you for everything. You have been a good friend to me. Will you please post this letter for me?"

"Sure." Johann took the envelope. "We will see each other again."

"I count on that," Richard answered with a grin, swallowing down any more serious emotion. Now wasn't the time to get sentimental. On an impulse, he took out a faded photograph, scribbled a note onto the back side, and handed it to Johann. It showed a blond teenage boy with a huge grin, oblivious to the coming dangers of war, holding a fiery, not-too-happy-looking redhead about the same age.

"That's you and your youngest sister, right?"

Richard nodded. "In case...you know...will you send this to my family? Let them know how much I loved them?" He bit down on his lip and blinked to keep the tears from springing into his eyes.

Johann apparently fought the same battle against tears and rasped a short "Yes" before rushing out of the room, leaving Richard alone with his thoughts. Sadness swept over him, but no fear. Once the decision was made, his fear had diminished.

With a heaviness in his heart, off he went to the station. Karl and Richard boarded the last wagon of the train for their long trek back to the Russian taiga, about 500 miles from Lodz.

"At least we hibernated in the barracks," Richard joked as he glanced into the faces of his fellow soldiers. Young boys. Old men. Faces that lacked the hardness etched into them from having experienced too much. Some expressions remained enthusiastic, but most radiated anxiety and fear. A few patched-up wounded were sprinkled in between with a knowing glance in their otherwise fatalistic mien. Fresh troops, he thought, always had a different air about them.

The train gained speed and rattled along, passing miserable images of destruction, charred rubble haunted by the ghosts of their former occupants.

"Look," Karl said and pointed to a gaping black hole in the mountain ahead. The locomotive driving into the long tunnel soon filled it. Wagon after wagon had disappeared into the darkness when suddenly the mountain exploded with great force and buried the train inside the tunnel. Giant pieces of rock and earth were hurled high up into the air. Dust and debris rained on the surrounding area.

Richard felt the earth shaking violently, as the last few wagons derailed from the impact. Tumbling, rolling, jolting, skidding, they finally came to a halt.

Dumbfounded, his head aching from the bump, Richard took inventory of his battered body and decided he was still alive. Karl crawled over to check on him.

"That's it? We die in a train crash?" Richard groaned.

"You're not dead yet, but you will be if you don't move your ass out of here."

Richard shook his head. His eyes fluttered closed, as he struggled against the urge to curl up in a ball and fade away. Rest. But his stubborn friend shook him awake and commanded, "Out of here now!"

With Karl's help, he managed to crawl to the broken window and squeeze through. Two wagons lay scattered about the tunnel entrance that was nothing more than a muddy hill now. *Buried alive.* Mourning for his fellow soldiers had to wait. It didn't help anyone right now.

A few dozen men crawled about, each one more battered than the next. At least Karl seemed to have the situation under control. He pushed Richard forward. "We have to hide."

*Hide? From whom?* Richard's brain scrambled to form a coherent thought, but the searing pain in his side killed every attempt to focus. He couldn't get up, so he crawled, following Karl and about half a dozen other men to the thick underbrush.

Karl urged them forward, despite the pain, the dizziness, and the confusion. About fifteen minutes later, they heard voices shouting Polish words. Richard had always liked literature. His love for the written word had instilled a love of the language and thus he'd picked up quite a few Russian and Polish sentences during his time in the Wehrmacht.

"Search for survivors," the deep voice said.

"Why can't we kill them?

"Not yet. They might prove a good bounty."

Richard's stomach clenched and he sent a prayer to the sky for the fact that Karl had ruthlessly pushed them deep into the woods. Hopefully, a German unit would patrol the area soon and find them. Until then, they needed to stay out of harm's way.

It was only a short distance back to Lodz. On a good day they could have walked over in five or six hours; less if they sprinted. But this wasn't a good day. Most of the men nursed broken legs or deep cuts. Even Karl proved to be in a severe condition. Now that the adrenaline had left his body, he groaned in pain from his shattered arm. Richard himself had ripped open his side and possibly broken a few ribs, which made breathing painful and difficult. His whole body was one mass of throbbing pain.

The lack of proper care combined with the loss of blood slowly sucked the fight out of him. He lay on his back, slipping in and out of a disturbed sleep, and listened to the idle conversation of his comrades.

"I want to go home," one of the young recruits said with a voice near to tears. "In my home town, we all lived together in peace; got along very well, we all did. We had Jewish teachers and doctors. There was never a problem."

"True. Some of them didn't even know they were Jews until the whole Aryan certificate thing," Joseph said. "How did we ever get into such a senseless situation?"

"Who knew things would reach this level of insanity? Hitler promised to make Germany great again, and see where we are now," a man about forty years old said. "Personally, I think this war is a lost cause and the sooner it ends the better for everyone."

"Stop saying these defeatist things!" a young lad called Alex said. "Victory is ours. Our Führer has said so. And I for my part am proud to serve my Fatherland. I begged my mom to let me enlist, but she wouldn't let me until I turned seventeen. *Totaler Sieg!*"

Richard and Karl exchanged glances. The enthusiastic lad would soon have a conversation with reality. She tended to change one's view rather quickly.

"Total victory, my ass," Karl said. "You're a numbskull if you still believe that propaganda shit."

But Alex continued on like a dog with a bone. "The Slavs are an inferior race. I, for my part, am not toiling under the occupation of an inferior race for the rest of eternity."

Richard slipped back into a feverish dream. On the second day, he dreamed of a patrol coming for them and woke with a start. Judging by the excited look on the other men's faces it wasn't a dream. He primed his ears to pick up any sound the patrol made.

"*Tam,*" someone shouted.

*Enemy patrol.* Richard's mouth went dry and his muscles tightened as his brain captured the Polish expression for *Over there* and his breathing all but stopped when a group of men came straight in their direction. Habit overtook exhaustion and fever, as he aimed his trusted MP40 at the oncoming group.

He couldn't confirm a hit, but within seconds a tumultuous shooting ensued on both sides. It stopped as quickly as it had started when the Germans ran out of bullets.

# CHAPTER 10

Richard groaned with pain and he felt something warm running down his arm. His life flashed before his eyes. The beautiful girl from Baluty smiled at him with her big brown eyes. Mutter gave him a kiss on his forehead to say goodbye the day he joined the Wehrmacht. Lotte grinned and beckoned to him to join her in the water at their favorite lake in Berlin. Ursula and Anna giggled and painted their lips to go out to a dance. Then, Vater walked by and said, "Get up, my son. Stand up and lean on me." He reached out his hand but Richard could not grasp it.

*I want to live a bit longer. I want to be a man and know the delights of love.* He smiled at this extraordinary thought and turned around to see Karl get up and walk away.

"Don't go now, Karl," he called out to his friend. He heard an agonized groan.

"Is that you, Karl?" he asked, since he couldn't move.

"Yes. Are you alright?"

"I can't move."

"The damn partisans dragged us into their village, tied us up here, and promised us the gallows in the morning."

Richard shivered. He would have preferred to return to unconsciousness, but the knowledge of his impending death prevented it. Adrenaline pumped through his body, subduing the ache and the fear. He rocked his shackles. Nothing.

"Don't waste your breath. These guys know what they're doing," Karl whispered.

A person stepped in front of them and unloaded a gob of spit on Richard. The disgusting liquid trickled down his cheeks, but he chose to ignore it. What else could he do?

Polish curses peppered them like verbal bullets, and Richard was glad that he didn't understand most of it. But then a stone hit his shoulder and he screamed with pain. A shower of stones hurled down on the defenseless men. Karl screamed after a loud clonking sound and sagged against Richard.

"Karl, Karl, are you still with me?" Richard asked frantically, but no answer came. He turned his head to see a huge bleeding gash on his friend's forehead. "Don't you dare leave me alone, you hear me, asshole?" But not even the insult caused Karl to stir.

"What a sorry bunch," someone said. "This war will soon be over for the Germans. And we are on the winning side."

"I don't even remember freedom and peace. What will we do?" Another one laughed.

"I have a girl waiting for me."

"Don't be too sure of that, comrade," his companion teased and the others broke into laughter. "It's been a long war and a long wait."

"This one has passed." One man kicked at the body lying on Richard's other side. The young soldier moved his head to recognize Alex, the enthusiastic young lad.

"Let him rot. We'll string him up with the others in the morning. It'll be a nice surprise for the German patrols."

As the hours wore on, Richard dozed off in between the insults and attacks of the villagers.

"Let me have a look at them," a familiar female voice said. Richard opened one swollen eye, but his ears and his heart recognized the voice even before he saw her. The girl from Baluty.

"They're Germans, they deserve to be treated like animals."

"Nobody deserves this," she said with a resolute voice and huddled down to check on Karl and then on Richard. Her wonderful brown eyes connected with his as she gave him a sip of water. He'd never felt a stronger connection to someone than in that moment. Despite the pain of his wounds, warmth surged through his veins at the miracle of seeing her again.

She leant forward to stroke sweat from his fevered brow and whispered, "Hang on. I'm coming back for you." Then she disappeared like a stunning and merciful hallucination.

The hours wore on as darkness blanketed the village. *Why don't Stalin and Hitler just toss a coin and be done?* Richard thought in his desolation. *There won't be anything left to win at this rate.*

Suddenly Karl stirred.

Richard's heart jumped with joy. "You're awake, my friend. I was worried..."

"Can you tell my mom that I love her?" Karl's breathing came out ragged.

"Oh, no. You don't die on me. Not yet."

"My time's running out. Promise you'll do everything to get home and tell her?"

"I will." Richard angled his body to lean his shoulder against Karl's and give him comfort. "Thanks for everything my, friend. It was a wild ride."

Karl barked out a laugh. "It was." Then his breathing stopped as his suffering ended.

Tears streamed down Richard's cheeks as he closed his eyes.

* * *

"Wake up!"

A wonderful dream.

The shaking continued. "Wake up!"

It took a moment until his night vision adjusted to the dim moonlit village. It was *her* again, accompanied by a bull of a man in his early twenties.

"Is it really you? Or am I dreaming?" A frightening thought occurred to him. "Am I already dead?"

"You're not dead yet." She undid his shackles and grabbed his arm. "Get up. We don't have much time."

*Time?* Time was draining the life out of his body. He nodded, stifling a moan, and did his best to stand up, but his legs refused to serve. Between the two of them, they helped Richard up and the burly man cast him over his shoulder to walk away from the marketplace harboring his dead comrades.

"Are you sure you want to do this, Katrina?" the man asked. "He's a German. Do you know what our people will do to you both if they find out you are sheltering the enemy?"

*Katrina. What a beautiful name for a beautiful girl,* Richard thought, bouncing up and down on the man's shoulders with every step he took.

"I have no choice but to pay my debts and save this man's life as he saved mine," Katrina replied. "Not a word of tonight's actions will ever escape my lips, you can be sure of that."

The man mumbled something under his breath that Richard couldn't understand. About half an hour later they reached a farmhouse and he dumped Richard onto a bed, before he disappeared into the misty dawn.

# CHAPTER 11

The following days passed in a blur. Richard lay in bed and Katrina came every couple of hours to tend his wounds or feed him. He saw how she crushed cabbage leaves with clean water to make a paste, which she applied to his wounds before she dressed them. Before long, he yearned for her gentle touch and kind words.

After a week, or perhaps two, Richard finally felt strong enough to venture out of his room. But before he could put the plan into action Katrina entered his room carrying a bowl of soup.

"Good morning, Katrina," he greeted her with a smile.

"You're feeling better, Richard."

"How do you know my name?"

Her cheeks turned a sweet pink and she pointed at his clean uniform, neatly folded across a chair. "I took the liberty of searching your pockets before washing it."

Richard moved his hands beneath the blanket to find the

familiar material of underwear missing and clamped his eyes shut as a wave of embarrassment washed over him. He'd rather not know who undressed him and preferred to believe it was the burly man he faintly remembered carrying him here.

"You need to eat," Katrina said in flawless German, holding out the bowl of soup for him.

"Thank you…" Richard started his sentence, but she'd already fled the room, leaving him stupefied and missing her company even before the last glimpse of her backside disappeared.

He ate his soup and then eyed his uniform with disdain. It stood for something he didn't want to be part of anymore, but since he had nothing else to wear, he slipped on the trousers and the jacket. Then he ventured out into the house. Upstairs were two more tiny bedrooms, similar to the one he'd been sleeping in. As far as he could tell, only one room was occupied – by Katrina – whereas the other one stood empty.

With wobbly legs, he descended the stairs into the big kitchen with the adjacent sitting room. A typical farmhouse. The outhouse stood several dozen yards away in the vegetable gardens, where hens were running around clucking. From what Richard could see this had once been a large working farm, growing crops and raising livestock.

"Eek," Katrina shrieked at the sight of him and jumped backward. "Oh, it's you. Sorry."

"It's the uniform, isn't it?" Richard asked and she nodded. It stabbed at his heart to know he'd scared her. It was easy to see how much she hated what his uniform represented. His country, his compatriots, his everything. He hadn't given it much thought before, but her reaction showed him that he couldn't walk around in this uniform. "I...maybe I should go back upstairs..." Richard turned, but his weak body protested, and he managed no more than four stair steps before he had to sit down, dizziness threatening to overwhelm him.

"Are you alright?" Katrina came and kneeled in front of him saying, "You look pale."

"I guess I overestimated my strength. I should return to bed." He tried a grin, but it probably looked more like a pain-ridden grimace.

"Why don't you sit here in the armchair and we'll chat while I get some work done?" She helped him up and led him to the comfortable armchair by the fireplace. During winter the fire would be a cozy place, but in late spring it lay idle.

"How long have I been here?" he asked, watching her chop green leaves.

"Eleven days," she said without looking up. Chop. Chop. Chop. With breathtaking speed, the knife in her hand cut through her supply of leaves.

"That long?" He lapsed into thought. By now they must have found the bodies of Alex and Karl. His heart squeezed with grief. How could he explain to his superiors where he'd been since the tunnel explosion? So much time had passed. He remembered well the interrogation and resulting lock-up in Warsaw. He had no reason to think it would be different this time.

What should he tell them when asked who'd nursed him

back to health? They would come for Katrina – he was sure about that. He couldn't risk her getting hurt because of him. *I'll have to disappear. Hide somewhere.*

"You can't return," she said, interrupting his thoughts. Then she turned her head and her warm brown eyes locked with his. "It wouldn't be safe. For either one of us." Her hands stopped chopping and poured the leaves into a big bowl.

"I know. I'll leave. Hide somewhere."

"First your strength has to return. You didn't even get up the stairs, how do you think you'll fare walking into the woods?"

"I hadn't thought about that. What are you doing?" he asked, pointing at the bowl.

"I'm making an ointment for your wounds. My parents..." she paused for a moment, "they were healers. They taught me about natural remedies."

"They're dead." It was an affirmation, not a question. He had heard the pain in her voice when she'd mentioned them and therefore wasn't surprised when she nodded. "Do you have siblings?"

"I do. Three brothers, all older than I am."

"Please tell me about them, if it's not too much to ask."

Katrina smiled in a way that lit up his heart. "Only if you tell me about your family, too."

"It's a deal." He chuckled. "But start by telling me why your German is so perfect."

"Actually, many people around here speak German. Before the invasion, we lived in peace with our neighbors. Jews, Germans, Poles, Ukrainians, Russians, everyone. We learned German and Russian at school, English too, because my parents thought languages are important."

"I agree with them," Richard said. "When we first met, I thought you didn't understand me."

"I refuse to speak German with the occupiers. They don't deserve it. And it's better to let them think I don't understand." Katrina kneaded the chopped leaves into a paste with a strong-smelling liquid.

"Where are we, by the way? In Baluty?"

"No, this farm is about a twenty-minute drive to Lodz. Not that we have motorized vehicles anymore...three hours' walk if you take the main road."

"But you live on your own? What about your brothers?"

"Currently, I'm the only one here." She sighed before continuing, "My oldest brother Piotr left for Warsaw to marry when he turned eighteen, twelve years ago. He became an officer in the Polish Army. He and his wife Ludmila used to visit us often, together with their son Janusz. Until the invasion. Since then I haven't heard from him. God only knows if he's still alive." She paused for a moment, scrambling for words. "Then there are Stanislaw and Jarek. They're twins, but they couldn't be more different from each other. They're still around. Somewhere."

By the way her voice grew wary he knew she was hiding something. Her brothers probably belonged to the partisans. Maybe they were responsible for blowing up the train tunnel, or his capture. He'd rather not meet them eye-to-eye.

"And then there's me. I'm the youngest. But since I'm the only one left on the farm, I do what I can to keep things running. The Germans have requisitioned everything of value and still they come back every now and then to demand more."

"It's a heavy burden on the shoulders of a young girl." Katrina was so fragile, yet so strong. His heart pounded his admiration for her.

She sent him an angry stare in response. "We do what we must. And nobody would be in this awful situation if it weren't for your awful Führer and his delusional racist ideas!"

"I'm sorry. I didn't mean to insult you. This…" he made a gesture encircling the room and taking in the world beyond it, "…I could have done without all of this. We were happy. My family and me. We didn't want this war either."

"Let's pretend the invasion never happened and our nations are still friends," she said, the smile returning to her face. "Now it's your turn to tell me about your family."

"I haven't seen them in almost two years. Since…since the day I turned seventeen and got my marching orders. My father was drafted in 1940 and all we know is that he's a prisoner of war somewhere in Russia."

"I'm sorry about that." Katrina's voice was full of compassion.

"My mother and two of my three sisters live in Berlin. Ursula, the oldest, works as a prison guard."

"Prison guard?" Her head whipped around.

"Not by choice. She was assigned this job by the *Reichsarbeitsdienst*. Ursula would never raise her voice to oppose or complain. So she obeyed. In contrast, Anna, the second one, fought tooth and nail to convince my parents to allow her to go to university and become a biologist. But she had to resign herself to becoming a nurse."

"A nurse. So we're basically colleagues." She held out the bowl to him. "Can you help me with this and pour it into the jars over there?"

"Sure." They worked together in silence, and cold sweat broke out on his forehead from the effort. Katrina was right; he wouldn't be able to leave the house, not before another three or four days of recovery.

"You said there's another sister," Katrina mentioned later as she closed the lids of the jars.

Richard returned to the armchair and flopped down with a groan. "Yes. Lotte. She's seventeen."

"Like me."

"In fact, you do remind me of her," he said with a chuckle as his mind drifted back to home. "She's fiery, strong-minded, outspoken, always taking risks. Our mother was so worried about her dislike for the Nazi government that she sent her to the country to live with our aunt."

A bell-like laughter filled the room. "The way you describe her, I'm sure we would become friends. Your sister and I."

"I guess you would. I miss her. A lot." He rubbed his scruffy face, suddenly feeling the weight of the entire world draped over his shoulders. "I should get back to bed."

"You should," she said after a scrutinizing glance at his face. "The fever is returning. Get some rest. I'll bring you another bowl of soup later."

Richard nodded and turned to go, but in the doorjamb, he turned around. "Perhaps you could give me something else to wear. If you have anything. It's not safe for either one of us if anyone sees me in my uniform."

"I'll check."

Panting, he made his way up the stairs, stopping every four steps and then dropped onto the bed, passing out within seconds.

When he woke, the sun had dipped low on the horizon and voices drifted to his room from downstairs. He slid to the door to close it, when he noticed a boy about eleven years old, with ruffled dark hair. Richard pressed against the wall, not daring to make a single sound for fear of being discovered.

"Tadzio, what can I do for you?"

"Ma was wondering if you might have something for Lola's gripes. Keeps us up all night with her crying," the boy said.

"I sure do," Katrina said, gesturing for Tadzio to follow her into the kitchen, away from the stairs. "Come on in and have some herbal tea while I mix Lola's medicine. It takes babies a while to settle down, you know."

Richard wondered if it wasn't simply hunger that made the poor mite howl. From what he'd seen, the Poles didn't get to keep much food for themselves.

"I set some traps today," the boy said, walking into the kitchen. "I'll come by tomorrow if I have any luck."

"Hmm, that would be nice, if you have anything to spare."

Richard silently closed the door and returned to his bed. Katrina had so much more on her hands than he could ever manage. Overwhelmed by an intense emotion for her, he determined to stay with her and help. *That makes me officially a deserter.*

The thought should frighten him. Make him feel guilty. Shameful, at least. Instead, relief flowed over him like a freshwater stream. Hitler's war wasn't his war anymore. Nobody could force him to commit or condone the atrocities happening. Freedom hovered just at the tips of his fingers.

## CHAPTER 12

The next day Katrina brought him trousers and a shirt. "They belonged to my brother Piotr. I didn't have the heart to give the clothes away, hoping he would one day come back to wear them." She left him to put them on and then laughed when he entered the kitchen.

"Your brother must be a big and muscular man," he said, pointing at the oversized trousers that hung from his hips.

"He is." She giggled and rushed away to come back with suspenders. "Here. Use these." She helped him fasten them on the trousers and he leaned – just a bit – into her touch. With every passing minute he grew fonder of this wonderful woman, and he sought out every opportunity to be near her, to touch her. Nothing inappropriate, of course. She wasn't that type of girl and he was sure she'd slap him in the face if he became impertinent.

"How do I look?" He grinned after giving a turn like a silly adolescent girl. Feeling carefree and silly for a change, he allowed himself to forget about his troubles for just a moment.

"Like a Polish peasant."

"Wait." He looked deep into her caring eyes. "I want to thank you for everything you've done for me. You've risked your life to save mine."

"It was nothing," she said, a charming blush coloring her cheeks a rosy hue.

"Yes, it was. And I want to give back at least something." He grasped her hand between his. "If you agree, I want to stay and help you with the farm, and with whatever else you're doing."

Katrina bit her upper lip, an internal war apparent in her expression. "You'll have to learn Polish to blend in."

"Actually, I happen to be quite proficient in your language," he said with pride.

"Let's hear."

He muttered a few sentences until her giggles drowned his voice.

"The words might be correct, but your accent gives you away. You'd better stay mute around people."

Richard shrugged. He'd do anything just to stay with her. For a magical moment, neither one of them moved, hesitant to destroy the strong connection holding them captive. Richard moved first, reaching out to wrap his arms around her. For a long minute they stood intertwined, content to be in each other's company, two souls bonded together against the rest of the world. When she raised her head to look at him, the ground moved beneath his feet and with trembling knees he pressed a kiss to her soft lips.

He'd had no idea. A single kiss and the world stopped spinning.

* * *

Richard started out helping in the house for an hour or two, but as the days passed he regained his strength and took on the heavy work in the fields. Fortunately the farm lay far enough away that visitors rarely came by, except for the young boy called Tadzio.

A city boy all his life, Richard's only experiences with farming had been the short visits with his aunt Lydia. But Katrina proved a patient teacher and he soon got the hang of it. He soaked up her knowledge the same way he'd soaked up words and wisdom from the books in his boyhood. Always trying to keep up with her, he proved she could count on him, making her forget that he was the enemy.

Katrina and Richard were busy sowing, planting, weeding, and caring for the hens and rabbits. Life as a farmer was hard work, but Richard didn't mind. It was a nice change to create instead of destroy. And he enjoyed the spring that warmed the days as plants sprouted, bringing color and a sense of life to the devastated country.

He considered burning his uniform, but then decided to keep it, just in case. With the uniform safely hidden away, his frantic mind settled, blocking out the horrors of war. Looking at Katrina as she prepared a salad from leaves, stalks, and buds they had collected earlier, he forgot about everything else.

"Hmm, that smells delicious, what is it?"

"Wild garlic, but we won't fill our bellies with green

leaves alone. Come, I'll show you the best place to catch crayfish around here." She grabbed a fish trap and put on her boots.

Hand in hand they walked the few hundred yards to the forest and then followed a small winding path for about an hour, before Richard heard the gurgle of running water. Stepping onto a clearing, he saw the clear creek cutting through lush grass and a tiny cascade disgorging water into a pond the size of a lorry.

"Take off your shoes," she said, unlacing her boots, shaking them off, and pulling off her socks. They walked with bare feet into the chilly pond and, under Katrina's vigilant eye, he learned how to set the crayfish trap. "We'll wait an hour or so and see what we've got." Katrina returned to the clearing and flopped backwards into the grass, exposing her face to the warm rays of sunshine while wiggling her toes. "Don't you just love how spring seems to bring back life to the earth?"

"I do. This happens every year when Persephone returns to live with her mother on earth," he said, following suit. Katrina put her head on his shoulder and he twisted a strand of her brown hair around his finger.

"Another Greek myth?"

"Yes. Want me to tell you?" In the long days of his recovery they'd sat for many hours in her kitchen and he'd started telling her about all the books he'd read in his childhood.

She snuggled closer to his side, warming his body from the inside, the same way the sunshine did from the outside.

"Demeter was the goddess of earth, agriculture, and fertility. One day, Hades, the god of the underworld, fell in love with her daughter Persephone and abducted her into the underworld. Demeter became so sad that nothing grew on earth anymore. Plants, animals, and ultimately humans withered away, deprived of the fertility Demeter had so generously showered our planet with. Ultimately, Zeus intervened to save the world and forced Hades to return Persephone to her mother. But since Persephone had already eaten in the underworld, she was bound there. In the end they agreed on a compromise: Persephone would live with her mother on earth half of the year, and the other half with her husband Hades in the underworld. Since then, nature goes into recess as Demeter mourns for her daughter to return in six months."

"That's a nice legend," Katrina said, turning around to look into his eyes. Richard couldn't resist, but had to pull her onto him and kiss her soft lips. Blood rushed to his groin as he felt her light weight on his body, and his hands roamed up and down her back.

Much later they returned to the trap and found it teeming with crayfish and the odd fish. Katrina used pliers to throw the big ones with a loud thud into her bucket and returned the small crayfish into the pond.

After everything he'd been through, he almost couldn't believe it possible.

Life was good.

# CHAPTER 13

After returning to the farm, Katrina prepared the crayfish to eat with the salad, while Richard chopped wood for the range.

"Dinner is ready," she called out.

"Coming," he shouted back, wiping the sweat from his forehead with the back of his hand.

He looked at Katrina and how she gracefully set the table and thought she was the most beautiful girl on earth. It was impressive how she managed to prepare filling, delicious meals day after day from not much more than wild plants and trapped animals. Some days, like today, she added an egg or two from the two remaining hens.

"This tastes so good, Katrina, I don't know how you do it," Richard said, spearing another bite on his fork. "Reminds me of home. You'd love my mother and sisters. Maybe one day we can all be together." Usually he forbade himself thoughts of the future; everything seemed too bleak and uncertain.

"How could I not love your family, Richard?" Katrina replied. "I never had sisters. What a joy it would be to have not one, but three sisters." She noticed the frown of sorrow on his forehead and put her hand over his. "We have to have faith."

"I do. Sometimes. But other times…" Richard broke off. It didn't make sense to burden her with his qualms. "You remind me so much of my sister Lotte. Strong-willed and stubborn as a mule."

"Is that so?" Katrina laughed.

A heavy knock on the door interrupted them and they looked at each other with anxiety in their eyes. These days, visitors were rarely friends.

"Hurry, hide in the lumber room," Katrina said and pushed him toward the hidden trap door.

Richard wanted to protest. Since when did he need to be protected by a woman? It should be the other way around. But she knew him well enough and gave him a stern glance, together with a wave of her hand, before she closed the trap door behind him. The incessant pounding continued as she walked toward the front door to open it.

Huddled in the tiny place beneath the kitchen floor, Richard strained his ears and soon enough heard footsteps. Light ones. That was Katrina. Heavy ones. A man. With boots. And another set of heavy footsteps. The rhythm sounded familiar. A German voice. Soldiers.

Trapped in the hideout, unable to open the door from the inside, he balled his hands into fists. If the German soldiers wanted to harm Katrina, there was nothing he could do but wait and listen.

And pray.

The voice explained they had come to requisition food. A sigh escaped his throat. Two soldiers and a beautiful girl alone – it could have been worse. This kind of random requisitioning wasn't officially allowed and a soldier caught doing it would be thrown into the lock-up for their trouble. But who would dare to report them? Certainly not the Polish civilians. They didn't go near the barracks or the administrative headquarters without being summoned.

Light footsteps again, followed by the heavy ones. Frantic squawking. Flapping of wings. A satisfied braying laughter. Opening and closing of cupboards. Voices, where he couldn't understand the words. Footsteps. The heavy front door slamming. Silence.

Several long moments later, Katrina returned and opened the trap door. He climbed out and took her into his arms.

"They took the chickens, the rabbits, and all the potatoes." She didn't cry, but he could feel her small body trembling with despair – and rage.

"We'll make do. Somehow," Richard assured her, although he had no idea how they were to eat with the stock of potatoes gone. And the chickens that reliably laid several eggs each week.

When he looked up, he saw the boy, Tadzio, standing in a confrontational pose, aiming his slingshot at him. Richard froze in shock. Katrina must have noticed, because she turned in his arms.

"Tadzio! Don't. He's a friend."

The boy didn't seem convinced and kept his rigid stance. "I heard the crazed hens squawking and saw the Germans, so I came here to check on you."

Katrina slipped out of Richard's embrace and approached the boy to press a kiss on his forehead. "Thank you so much, big man. The soldiers are gone. They took our animals and a sack of potatoes."

"Shall I go after them?" Tadzio asked, broadening his stance, completely convinced an eleven-year old equipped with a slingshot could take it up with two grown – and armed – men.

"No. We'd better not stir up a ruckus, don't you think?" Katrina put a hand on his arm. "I'm so thankful that you look out for me."

Tadzio beamed with pride, but then his glance fell upon Richard and his expression darkened. "Who's that? I've never seen him before."

"This is Richard," Katrina answered without thinking.

"Richard?" Tadzio spat out the name. "A German? How can you make common cause with *them?*"

"It's not like that." Katrina looked frantically between the two males. "He saved my life, back in Baluty. If it had not been for Richard, I would not be alive today."

Tadzio squinted his eyebrows. "That doesn't explain why he's here."

Richard stepped up. "My train was derailed when the tunnel exploded–"

"That was a good job done by our boys." Tadzio beamed again.

"It was," Richard had to admit. "I was wounded and destined to be hanged." Tadzio scrunched up his nose at the mention. "Katrina saved me, and nursed me back to health. I decided to stay and help her run the farm."

Tadzio cocked his head. "That would make you...a

Wehrmacht soldier?" The boy hopped up and down, "Oh my God! You're a deserter! A German deserter. Now I know we will win this war for sure."

Both Richard and Katrina had to chuckle. For a child, things were either black or white. The complications of the infinite gray tones in between only came with adulthood.

"You won't turn him in, will you?" Katrina begged.

"I don't think I will." Tadzio put on a serious face, before he continued, "As long as he doesn't harm you. If he does, let me know and he's history."

"I promise never to hurt Katrina," Richard said, stretching out his hand to the boy. Tadzio shook it and looked very pleased with himself.

* * *

It hadn't been easy after the chicken fiasco, but looking at the bright side, Richard had come to like Tadzio. They bonded like brothers and spent much of their time together doing odd jobs around the farm, for which Katrina always rewarded the boy with food to bring home to his mother and two sisters. Since his father had been killed in battle, Tadzio was the man of the house and did his best to provide for his family.

Katrina and Richard were spading the field behind the farm, a grueling task that had been done with an ox before the war. Sweat dripped from Richard's forehead and ran down his back in rivulets. He straightened his spine and looked up into the spring sun. The blazing orb stayed high in the sky and burned down on them with an unexpected force. For a fleeting moment he wished for the chilly winter gusts.

He gulped down a bowl of water from the well and then offered some to Katrina. She straightened her back, giving him one of her beautiful smiles, and, like it always did, his heart missed a beat. This beautiful woman looked so delicate, but she had the strength and resilience of an ox. He couldn't resist and pulled her into an embrace that ended in a heated kiss.

"We need to continue." She sighed, slipping out of his arms. It was high time to sow and plant the field if they wanted to eat this coming winter. Richard had never before appreciated how hard farmers worked and how their lives revolved around the seasons of the year. In Berlin two days of rain meant the nuisance of wet feet and muddy streets, but here it could mean the difference between food or starvation.

"Yes." He took the bar spade with his blistered, hurting hands and dug into the earth again. Katrina followed in his trail, sowing, planting, watering.

Hours later, a figure appeared, walking down the road to the farmhouse. Richard stopped his work for a moment to squint his eyes at the visitor. "It's Tadzio," he said with relief.

The boy came rushing into the backyard, waving one hand, while the other one held tight onto a sack over his shoulder. "I was at the crossroads all day selling berries to passers-by and I heard interesting accounts about the war. It seems it's just a matter of months, days in fact, before a cease-fire is going to be declared."

"Selling berries?" Richard laughed. "You're such an optimist, Tadzio. Who has money to buy berries here? As for the rumors, don't believe a word you hear."

"People do stop and give me a few pennies for my fruit," Tadzio said with a self-important expression on his face.

"How much did you earn?" Katrina giggled at the audacity of the young boy.

"Enough to buy these two from the man who had his baskets where I sat." Tadzio grinned and opened the sack. "For you, Katrina." He added shyly and Richard acknowledged that he wasn't the only one enamored with the lovely girl.

"Chickens," Katrina exclaimed and grabbed the frenzied hen to set it into the empty enclosure. "Thank you so much, but you should have used your money to buy food for your mom."

A sly grin crossed his face. "I bought two, and I give you one in exchange for taking good care of my hen and giving me her egg,s."

"It's a deal then," Katrina shook his hand. She knew that Tadzio's house and garden were much too small to raise a hen, while she had the space. "You're the best little brother in the world." Her compliment thrilled the innocent youngster, who blushed a bright red and shrugged awkwardly.

"You will forget about me when your real brothers come back," he said, his eyes misting up.

Richard knew that Katrina was anxiously awaiting news about Stanislaw and Jarek, since she hadn't heard anything of them for weeks now. He put his arms around her. "Your brothers are going to show up soon. I bet they are just fine."

"They've never been away for such a long time. Ever

since they blew up the train tunnel—" She clapped a hand in front of her mouth. "I'm sorry."

"Don't be sorry. They're just doing what they must. We all do awful things in this war." Richard swallowed. He'd long suspected that the tunnel explosion had been the work of the resistance, but hearing that Katrina's own brothers were involved in killing his comrades clutched at his heart. Karl entered his mind, and tears threatened to spill. But he wouldn't allow himself the weakness of weeping in front of a woman and a boy.

Then another, frightening, thought entered his mind. What would happen if her brothers indeed showed up at the house? They would not be pleased to find a German there.

# CHAPTER 14

The next day after darkness had settled over the Polish flatlands, Richard heard scratching sounds from the kitchen. Alarmed, he grabbed the bat by his bedside and snuck downstairs. But before he reached the ground floor, strong arms grabbed him and one big hand was pushed over his mouth.

Richard kicked at his attacker, but stopped at the distinctive click of a safety being released on an MP40, the standard German infantry weapon. While he racked his brain over whether he should identify himself as a German or not, someone flashed a lantern into his face. In the short moment the light swept across the room before blinding him, he caught a glimpse on the clothing of the submachine gun holder. Definitely not Wehrmacht. So the weapon was booty.

"What's going on down there? Richard?" Katrina's voice sent a hot wave of relief through Richard's veins, followed by icy chills of fear. Moments later Katrina came down with a lantern and Richard got a good view at the man holding him at gunpoint. A filthy man with broad shoulders, dark hair, and a full beard covering his face. The rifle definitely was German, but the shabby clothing was Polish – Home Army.

"Katrina? Are you alright?" one of the men asked.

"Stan! Jarek! I was so worried about you." She dashed down the stairs. "Put away your gun, Richard's a friend."

Reluctantly the man lowered his gun and enfolded his sister into a bear hug, but the other man still held Richard's arm behind his back and covered his mouth. Only when Katrina turned and gave the man in Richard's back a lethal stare did he release his grip.

"*Dziękuję,*" Richard thanked, rubbing his hurting shoulder.

"Have you lost your mind, sister? Who's that bastard with the German name and accent?"

"Come into the kitchen, you must be hungry," Katrina said and led the way to the range, where the embers still glowed.

Jarek, or Stan, shoved Richard into the kitchen, never once letting him forget about the submachine gun ready to point at him. Katrina warmed a hearty soup with a few potatoes they'd found earlier when spading the field. She added generous pieces of a wild rabbit trapped a few days ago. The smell of food seemed to mollify her brothers enough to sit down at the table, hanging their guns on the backs of their chairs.

Richard thought it best to disappear, but when he slid out of the kitchen, one of the brothers called him back.

"German bastard. You stay here where I can see your hands."

"Stop calling him names. He's a good man," Katrina intervened, serving big bowls of steaming soup to her brothers.

"He's a Fritz."

"So why's he here?" the other one, with a long and ugly scar across his cheek, asked.

"He's here because he needed a place to stay and I needed help with the farm, Jarek."

*So this is Jarek.* Apart from the scar, the two men looked identical.

Stan shoved his half-empty bowl away and growled, "You could have told us, if you needed help."

"Told you? I haven't seen you in weeks. For all I know, you could have been dead by now." She stared at her brother. "You do your job and let me do mine."

Jarek seemed less hot-tempered ,than his twin and spooned his soup in silence, before he leaned back and held out his bowl to Katrina. "That's fantastic, sister, can I have more?"

She smiled at the compliment and refilled his bowl. "You want some, too, Stan?"

Stan gave a growl and a nod, and then dug into his food like it was his first hot meal in days. Once he finished eating, he stared with blatant animosity at Richard. "The Fritz has to leave."

"No," Katrina said, putting her fists on her hips.

"Are you bats, Katrina?" Stan all but shouted at her with a crimson red face. "He's a bloody German. He will not spend another minute in this house. In fact he should not

97

spend another minute on this earth." Stan's hand shot back to grab his MP40.

"Put down your gun at once or shoot me first!" Katrina shielded Richard with her body. "Please stop being so driven by hate, and hear what I have to say."

"We could listen first and shoot him later," Jarek said with a chuckle.

Richard hated the way they talked as if he weren't in the same room with them. He felt sorry for Katrina, who had to endure the harsh judgment of her brothers, and he feared for his life. From what Richard had seen so far, Stan's temper had a short fuse and he knew how to handle his submachine gun. At this distance, the weapon would turn him into a shredded mess.

"Richard's a good man. He saved me from being raped and possibly murdered by his fellows back in Baluty."

"And you paid the debt by giving him exclusive rights to your body?" The veins on Stan's neck pulsated with rage. "Shame on you for consorting with the enemy. You both deserve to be shot for the disgrace you have brought on our family!"

Richard couldn't keep his mouth shut any longer. "I did not sleep with your sister. And I would never force myself upon a woman. Ever."

"How...how could you think so little of me?" Tears of fury rolled down her cheeks and she showered her brothers with a salvo of rapid-fire Polish words Richard didn't understand. They argued back and forth, too fast for him to understand most of it, but in the end, her brothers reluctantly agreed that Richard could stay in the farmhouse – for now.

"How long will you stay?" Katrina finally asked them.

"I'm afraid we have to leave before dawn. It's too dangerous to be seen around here. Your Fritz's compatriots have put a bounty on our heads."

Katrina embraced each one of them for a long minute, before she climbed upstairs to prepare the third bedroom for them to sleep in. As soon as she slipped out of sight, Stan closed the distance to Richard and said, "Listen carefully, Fritz. If you so much as touch my sister, I will take great pleasure in chopping off your hands and then make you die a slow and painful death. Understood?"

"Fully." Richard believed every single word Stan said and decided it wasn't a good time to confess that Katrina and he had kissed already.

# CHAPTER 15

When Richard woke before dawn, Katrina greeted him with dark shadows under her eyes from having stayed up all night to wash her brothers' clothes. In contrast to their usual morning routine, he didn't dare kiss her or even give her an embrace, as she finished stuffing their bags with food and extra clothing.

Instead he busied himself helping her set the table while she made breakfast. To celebrate the special day, she raided the weekly ration of eggs from the new hen and even took a piece of sausage from the hidden pantry beneath the kitchen floor.

Stan and Jarek came downstairs several minutes later, and, after giving mean side-glances at Richard, recounted the rumors about the upcoming closure of the Lodz Ghetto and the deportation of everyone living there.

"It's true. The Wehrmacht has been tasked to secure transport to resettle everyone to the East," Richard admitted.

"To death camps, you mean." Stan sneered as he clipped out each word. "Resettlement means a gas chamber if you're lucky or being worked to death at one of your camps, eh, Richard?"

Richard turned white as a sheet, not willing to believe that Stan was confirming his worst suspicions. "That can't be true. Why would they do that?"

"Your good German is just like every one of those rats," Stan said, facing Katrina, and then sneered at Richard again. "Are you really that dim-witted or are you merely protecting your sadistic compatriots?"

"No, no…" Richard shook his head, but Stan steamrolled over him. "Have you ever wondered how someone can survive on half the rations a Pole gets, which is less than a German gets? Have you ever asked yourself why nobody ever returns from one of the camps? Have you seen the skeletons clad in rags, doing the work of an ox?"

Richard felt the blood drain from his head as he listened to Stan explaining in vivid color the destiny of the Jews under the German occupation. The glimpses he'd seen suddenly all fell into place. Shame for his nation spread through his body and reddened his cheeks.

"I…I didn't know." He lumped back in his chair, pushing the half-eaten breakfast away.

"Now you do," Jarek chimed in, "and what will you do about it? Sit here and feel sorry for yourself?"

"Let him be," Katrina said, but her intervention only agitated her brothers even more.

"You're not even man enough to stay with your army. You deserted to save your own skin, because you know that

Germany will lose this war, and soon!" Jarek bellowed. "You are a filthy coward, that's what you are!"

Richard didn't think he was a coward. Naïve yes, stupid perhaps, but never a coward. He had volunteered for the front because he couldn't stand witnessing more of the SS's atrocities committed against civilians. But he chose not to mention this; it wouldn't help to calm Stan's and Jarek's hate. In their vengeful eyes, his German heritage painted him a criminal without the benefit of judge or jury.

"Every single damn German is a cog in the machine bull-dozing over Europe killing millions and millions."

"You're right," Richard said, stunning Jarek into silence. Three heads whipped around and three pairs of eyes shot open at his confession. "I was a cog in the German war machine, but I'm not anymore. I want to do my part to stop this madness." The words tumbling out of his mouth shocked him just as much as they did the three Poles. When had he made the jump from fugitive deserter to offering to play an active part in the Polish resistance?

Katrina regained her composure first. She poured everyone a special herb brew that tasted almost like coffee and said, "I'm worried about Agnieska."

"Who's that?"

"Agnieska is our sister-in-law. Her sister Ludmila was married to Piotr, our oldest brother, the one who's been missing since the invasion," she explained with a tired voice. When she didn't offer any more explanation, Jarek continued for her, "Agnieska and Ludmila are Jews."

Richard barely dared to ask his next question. "Where are they now?"

"Where do you think, Fritz?" Stan drew his eyebrows together. "In the Lodz Ghetto, of course."

"Piotr sent the two women and his son Janusz to live with us on the farm before the war broke out, because he thought they'd be safer here than in Warsaw. But..." Katrina had difficulties controlling the tremble in her voice. "...the three of them were forced to move to the Ghetto three years ago. About a month later we received news that Ludmila had died of fever..." At the last part, her voice abandoned her.

"Two years ago all children were deported to Chełmno. Gassed. All of them. Janusz was on the list." Stan fought against tears himself. "But for all we know, our sister-in-law is still alive."

"Not for long," Jarek added.

The threat of closing down the Ghetto and sending all occupants to a death camp hung over the small group like a dark thundercloud.

"Can't you get her out?" Richard asked and again three pairs of eyes stared at him as if he'd gone nuts.

"Are you crazy, Fritz? You think we can just walk inside, find her, and walk out?" Stan glared daggers at Richard, but Jarek tilted his head and murmured, "If we had a plan...we would need a plan...there must be a way..."

The energy in the room shifted and soon they were making plans about how to rescue Agnieska before the Ghetto would be closed down. In the end, they concluded that Stan and Jarek needed to make enquiries first.

# CHAPTER 16

Katrina and Richard returned to their usual routine, working the small farm. They had quotas to fill and sell to the Germans, feed themselves, and feed a group of resistance fighters hiding in the woods. Food was never enough, money was always scarce.

But they had each other, and despite the threats of doom hanging over them, they held on to the moments of happiness like holding on to dear life itself. The gift of a wildflower could brighten Katrina's face and earn Richard a kiss that made his insides melt and stirred his desire for her. As long as a whisper of hope remained, they would not succumb to the drabness of war.

Several days later, a bedraggled Stan staggered into the farmhouse at dusk without saying a word. Katrina led him to the kitchen table and filled his mug with hot herb brew from the stove. He sipped the liquid and stared with blank eyes at the wall.

"What happened? Where's Jarek? Did you find out about

Agnieska?" she asked, full of anxiety, but he wouldn't answer.

Richard recognized the lethargic, subdued look in Stan's eyes and feared the worst. He motioned for Katrina to stop asking questions and prepare dinner instead. She had saved meat from two squirrels Richard had trapped the day before, and added a generous portion to the potato and carrot stew on the range. After finishing his food, Stan buried his head in his arms and sobbed. Katrina rushed to his side to cuddle him like a crying baby.

Not wanting to embarrass Stan, Richard snuck out of the kitchen to busy himself in the backyard, herding the hens into the chicken coop for the night. He'd just securely locked the door against human or animal intruders when a high-pitched scream ripped through the silent night.

Richard dashed into the kitchen and saw a distraught Katrina pummeling her fists into Stan's chest, before she sagged into the armchair by the cold fireplace with puffy eyes.

"Jarek is dead," Stan explained.

Richard closed the distance and hugged the weeping Katrina, which earned him an ugly stare from her brother, but he couldn't care less. He held her in his arms, until she stopped crying and wiped her face with the back of her hands.

"What do we do now?" she asked in a low voice.

"Jarek found out that the rumors about closing the ghetto are true. The factories are training forced workers to take over the tasks of the Jews."

A shiver rolled down Richard's spine. Like everything in his country, even the extermination of a race had to be done according to a meticulously followed plan. The poor souls were forced to train their replacements before they would be sent to their deaths.

"We need to rescue Agnieska, we owe it to Jarek," Katrina said between sobs.

"Please don't act in haste," Richard advised. "The Ghetto is heavily secured and–"

"Who asked you, German swine?" Stan shouted. "Shut up. It's all your fault! If it weren't for your maniac Führer, Jarek would still be alive!"

"Richard is just trying to help." Katrina burst into tears again.

"Get him out of here, before I strangle the Hun with my bare hands." Stan stood up with clenched fists. He pierced Richard with his hatred while his body trembled with rage.

Richard raised his hands and backed out of the room. "Hey, calm down. I understand your pain, but I'm not the one who killed your brother."

"Doesn't matter. One German is as good as the next to pay for the sins of the many." Richard preferred not to respond and disappeared upstairs to his room. Much later he heard first Katrina and then Stan go to bed. Then he tiptoed downstairs to use the outhouse in the backyard. When he returned inside, he saw Stan standing in the kitchen with a grim face.

"I want you gone. I won't stand by and watch how you disgrace my sister," Stan said.

"I'm not–"

"Do you think me stupid? I see the way you two look at each other. Don't get up your hopes, bastard."

Richard felt the anger boil his blood. Stan might be hurt

and grieving, he might feel justifiable hate for everything German, but that didn't give him the right to spew his verbal vomit at Richard's feet. "Watch out. That's not your decision to make."

The next moment Stan's fist connected with his jaw, and Richard groaned with pain. "Shit," Richard muttered and let his fists fly. He didn't think as instinct took over. Instinct and incessant training. An in-close fight man-to-man was the last thing any soldier wanted, but that didn't mean he wasn't prepared for it. Over the buzz of adrenaline in his ears, Richard unleashed his pent-up emotions. Guilt, frustration, anger, hopelessness, fear. He embraced the madness and kicked, elbowed, punched, and struck, until he tasted blood.

The metal taste brought him to his senses. Stan wasn't the enemy. He dodged the next uppercut and yelled, "Stop it, Stan! I love your sister!"

Stan stood perplexed for a second, giving Richard the opportunity to put the large wooden table between the two of them. They circled each other around the table for a minute or two, when a drowsy voice yelled, "Both of you. Stop it now."

Katrina entered the kitchen, using herself as a human barrier between the brawlers. Richard glanced at her out of the corner of his eye, while he kept his focus on Stan, whose shoulders sagged as a whoosh of air left his lungs.

"Sorry, Kat," Stan mumbled and made to leave the room.

"You stay." Her command cut through the room like a knife through butter and both men snapped their heads toward her. For a moment, Richard feared Stan would go berserk against his sister and readied himself to launch at him. Katrina though wasn't in the least fazed and asked with a stern voice, "What on earth were you fighting about?"

Both of them shrugged, unwilling to tell her the truth.

Katrina waited and when no answer came, she said, "Well then. Don't tell me. But here's what I tell you. Both of you. Listen well and if you don't agree, leave my house—"

"It's my house, too," Stan objected.

"Shut up. As long as you have a bounty on your head, this is my house and mine alone. So if you wish to come here, you get along with Richard. Whether you like him or not, I don't care. But you will show him the respect any human deserves." She looked at Richard. "Same rules for you. Understood?"

"Yes, ma'am," Richard said with the most serious voice he could muster. She was too cute in her role as head governess scolding two dreadful boys.

"Whatever," Stan growled and went upstairs, slamming the door to his room.,

## CHAPTER 17

The next morning over breakfast Katrina announced that she wouldn't give up that easily.

"We've already lost so many family members, there must be a way to rescue Agnieska," she said into the silence.

"It's too risky." Stan chuckled at the indignant look she gave him. "You have to stay on the farm, because you're feeding not only yourself but my entire partisan unit. None of them could do their job without the food from this farm."

Richard didn't see eye to eye with Stan on many topics, but he couldn't argue that point. Her job might not be heroic or adventurous, but the resistance relied on her contribution to the effort. He cast his eyes downward onto his bowl of porridge, swallowing down a response that would surely rouse Stan's temper.

"I can't sit here and do nothing. If you're not willing to help, maybe Richard is. Any idea how we could get into the Ghetto?"

"We will not consult with our enemy," Stan spat out,

giving Richard a murderous stare. "How can you even be sure he won't run to the Wehrmacht headquarters and betray us in a desperate attempt to safe his own life?"

"Stop being childish, Stan. Richard might have some useful insight, and we need all the help we can get. The problem with you is that your emotions cloud your clear thinking, and one day we'll all get killed thanks to your short fuse."

"I am not working together with the Fritz. If you want me to be part of this, he," Stan nodded toward Richard before continuing, "stays out."

Richard thought it best to leave the quarrel to the siblings. They didn't want or need his help. Besides, he didn't have any useful advice to offer.

"I have work to do. See you around." Richard got up and laced his heavy boots with flying fingers before he walked outside. A part of him could understand Stan's hostility, but it still hurt. And made him question himself, his motives, his role in the German war machine.

Deep in thought he opened the hen coop, fed the newly acquired bunnies with grass, pumped water from the well, and then marched off toward the vegetable beds. Should he have known about the death camps? Could he have known? A soldier's main task was to obey orders, not to question intent. Usually the high command had a more complete, strategic view of things than the rank and file. Even if he had known, could he have done anything? Would he?

Richard kneeled down to weed the beds, tossing the plants into a bucket to give to the hens and rabbits later. Being honest with himself Richard knew he wasn't cut out from hero material. He was just an eighteen-year-old boy, prematurely turned into a man by war, who did what was expected of him. What did he know? Maybe Hitler was right, and the Jews really were the root of all evil? Maybe they had to be extinguished just like the weeds taking precious light and water from the vegetables. He wiped the back of the hand across his forehead.

Since when had things become so complicated? Back at home, he'd played with his friends, and hadn't even known whether they were Jews or not. Hadn't cared. Done with the weeding, he took up the spade to dig up another patch of land for planting potatoes. The farm work reminded him of the happy vacations he'd spent at Aunt Lydia's farm in Lower Bavaria, and he smiled at the memory of his first ever crush when he was twelve, or maybe thirteen.

Her family lived next to Lydia's. She was a cute brunette with the sweetest smile and he'd been smitten, but too shy to talk to her. Rachel Epstein was her name.

Epstein.

It hit him like one of Stan's fists between the eyes. Her family must be Jewish. He swallowed at the possibility of what had happened to her.

"Richard," Tadzio shouted and rushed down the road to join him.

"Hi, Tadzio, up so early?"

"Yes," the boy said with a proud expression. "I have to collect wood for the stove." Coal was hard to come by these days if you weren't German or at least *Volksdeutsch*, a Polish citizen of German ancestry.

"Help me here and I'll collect wood with you later," Richard offered and the boy beamed with joy. The hard work was only half as strenuous when it was shared.

"What happened to your eye?" Tadzio asked.

Richard touched his swollen skin, probably turning blue and black. "Stan's fist. He returned last night and blames me for his brother's death."

"Jarek is dead?" The shock blanched Tadzio's face.

"Yes. Captured during one of their missions."

Tadzio frowned, but then raised his fist. "He will be avenged! Soon the Home Army will slay the Germans, send them back to where they came from. I wish I was old enough to join up. I'd kill off the enemy in no time at all."

Richard stood frozen. The boy's enthusiasm for killing anyone German trickled down his spine like droplets of ice. Tadzio cast his eyes downward and flushed a rosy hue of regret. "Not you, of course. You're not really a German. You're nice."

For the umpteenth time Richard questioned his decision to stay with Katrina. Most everyone hated him, or would if they knew his true identity. He couldn't count on the empathy of the locals, but he couldn't return to his own people either. Not now. Maybe not ever. Danger lurked in every corner. Apparently, the question wasn't if he'd be killed, but who'd get to him first.

"Jarek was such a nice fellow. So kind and funny," Tadzio interrupted Richard's morose thoughts with his exuberant innocence not yet darkened by the horrors of killing his enemy. "He always had time for us kids and never let any of the big boys bully us. That was before..." Tadzio fought a losing battle against the tears forming in his eyes.

"Hey, enough talking, there's work to do," Richard said, tossing a spade at the boy. The physical strain and the fresh crisp air soon did their job, blotting out the blues. Soon enough curiosity and the fascination of all things war-related got the better of Tadzio and he asked, "You were at the front, right?"

Richard nodded.

"How was it?

"Cold." Richard had no intention of relaying the grimy details of combat to the boy. "You don't know cold until you've experienced a Russian winter." He grimaced and shivered involuntarily. "It was so long and hard. We sometimes froze to the earth when lying for hours in the trenches, waiting."

"Didn't your army keep you well supplied?"

"Nothing can withstand the Russian winter. In my first year we went into winter training, but last year, it was plain nuts. We froze our asses off. Literally. More than one of the boys got frozen to the thunderbox." Richard laughed. In hindsight it was funny. It hadn't been with pants down in sub-zero temperatures. "The Russians understood their winters. They wore fur-lined caps and gloves."

"So the weather was the real enemy." Tadzio grinned with a wisdom beyond his tender age. "And it defeated your great army."

"True enough," Richard agreed, resting for a moment on the handle of his spade. Sweat poured down his back and face. He wouldn't mind a bit of snow right now.

"Do you believe this war will be over soon? Everyone is talking about it."

"Honestly, I have no idea. Although I wish the rumors were true." Richard continued digging the heavy earth soaked from the rains of the last days. *Why on earth are we even fighting this war? Why can't we all just get on with our lives?*

He dug harder, trying to work off his guilt. Whenever he tried to grasp the sense of this madness, and his role in it, his head began to ache.

One of his favorite books in a previous life had been *All Quiet on the Western Front* by Erich Maria Remarque. The book depicted the story of a young soldier experiencing the horror and disillusionment of life in the trenches during the previous World War. Even then Richard had shared the protagonist's opinion. War was senseless. It was started by the rich and famous as they manipulated and hungered for even more wealth and power – men who'd never have to die at the front.

But at the same time he still felt guilty about deserting the Wehrmacht. His comrades, his superiors, they'd been good to him. It was like family. Although in Lodz he'd looked into the abyss of human cruelty. Waffen-SS. No way would he have any part in this. But maybe he should have returned, tried to fight the system from within instead of hiding on a farm.

# CHAPTER 18

The rain came pelting down and Richard dashed into the house. He took off his muddy boots at the entrance door and then turned around to see Stan and Katrina watching him.

"Um...Stan wants to ask you something."

"I need your uniform. Now," Stan demanded.

"Why on earth would you need my uniform?" Richard replied, taken aback at the peculiar request.

"None of your business, Fritz."

"Stan wants to walk into the Ghetto posing as a German soldier, and escort Agnieska out with him," Katrina explained hesitantly.

"That's your plan? Flimsy is an understatement. In fact, it's beyond ridiculous. Anyone can see you're not German from a mile away, and your picture on the wanted posters doesn't help either."

Stan sneered. "So you have a better plan?"

"I don't, but as much as you hate me, I can't let you rush

headlong into disaster." Richard didn't so much worry about Stan as he did about Katrina, who had just lost her other brother.

"We have to do something," Katrina insisted. "We have it on good authority that the deportations will start by the end of the month. If we don't act swiftly, Agnieska is dead."

"Even if he manages to get inside, he can't just escort her out of the Ghetto. There are rules, even for Germans. Haven't you read about that Wehrmacht officer who was caught red-handed with a Jewish girl in a hotel room? I believe both of them were executed for committing the capital crime of *Rassenschande*." Racial defilement – sexual relations between Aryans and non-Aryans – had been forbidden since the Nuremberg laws of 1935.

"So what would we need to get her out?"

Richard furrowed his brows. "A work permit? If you could get her a work permit in one of the ammo factories…"

"And where do we get this, know-it-all?"

Katrina thought aloud. "There's this man, he regularly buys our rabbits. He's *Volksdeutsch* and has a high-up position in the administration. We could ask him, but we still have the problem with the uniform and Stan."

A long silence ensued, where each one of them pondered their options.

"I will do it," Richard finally said.

"You?" Katrina and Stan said at once.

"At least nobody will mistake me for a Pole." Richard grinned, his heart beating frantically in his throat, fueled by both fear and excitement.

"But someone might recognize you," Katrina said, her voice quivering with worry.

"It's a risk I'm willing to take." The more Richard thought about the plan, the more confident he grew. He'd been in hiding for much too long; it was about time he returned to the action. Saving a life to make up for all the lives he'd extinguished.

"Agnieska doesn't know him. I should go. She'll trust me," Stan said. He was right. They couldn't risk Agnieska's making a scene or alerting someone. If she didn't know about the plan she might inadvertently expose Richard and herself.

Katrina shook her head. "No. You won't even get near the Ghetto before you're captured. There's a reason why you've been hiding in the woods."

"You could send a message to Agnieska..." Richard proposed.

"By mail? Or how exactly should we do this?" Stan couldn't stop bickering, but Richard had decided to ignore his attacks.

"Oh! I know!" Katrina hopped up and down. "Magda Lenska!"

"That might work." Stan's eyes brightened. "Yes, we will ask her to carry a message."

"Who exactly is this Magda Lenska?" Richard asked and a slightly mollified Stan deigned to favor him with an explanation. "She's the midwife around here. Has been for thirty years. She has a special permit to access the Ghetto."

"Do you trust her?" Richard didn't like the idea of having more confidants. The fewer people involved, the better. For everyone.

Both nodded enthusiastically.

"Stan, you will contact Magda and ask her to give Agnieska our message. I'll try to organize a work permit meanwhile, and then Richard will take it from there." Everyone nodded at Katrina's words.

\* \* \*

The next morning Stan left on his mission to contact the midwife.

"You will be careful, won't you?" Katrina embraced her brother and made him promise to come back alive. "I couldn't bear to lose you, too."

"Good luck, Stan," Richard said, extending his hand.

"Count on that." Stan half-grinned, ignored the outstretched hand, and stomped off.

As soon as Stan left, Richard kissed Katrina and held her tight. As always, the flame of desire kindled and he deepened the kiss. She opened her lips for him and the passion seeped in, blocking out all fear and anxiety, until she suddenly broke the kiss.

"Let's get to work," she said, her cheeks flushed in the sweetest pink. Richard's heart always squeezed tight when he observed her. That girl – woman actually – had endeared herself to him so much that just the thought of ever being separated again pained his soul. Throughout the day Richard kept his hands busy with the never-ending chores of a farmer, but as the night settled, an awkward shyness evolved between them. Both knew this wasn't just another adventure. The planned mission could well mean the death of everyone involved.

"I'm so worried about Stan," Katrina admitted over dinner.

"He'll do just fine. You'll see." Richard injected a confidence into his words he didn't feel. So many things could go wrong, had already gone wrong. He helped her wash the dishes and then they settled into the armchairs, Katrina mending socks, Richard mending fishing nets.

"Today one of the neighbors came by and inquired about you," she said.

"About me?"

"She's seen you working in the field. I told her you're a distant cousin from up North who has lost his home in the conflict. Your name is Ryszard Blach, by the way, because Richard Klausen won't go over very well." She smiled and his heart filled with love. "Up North they speak a dialect that sounds similar to the way your accent does." Richard's Polish had improved considerably over the past months, and he was fluent now. Even Tadzio had acknowledged his proficiency.

"Have you always lived around here?" he asked to dispel all worrisome thoughts.

"My great-grandparents came here from the Mazury. Back then this farm was at least ten times the size it is now. My parents both were healers with no interest in farm work, so they sold most of the land. We used to be well off…"

Richard put his fishing net away and touched her arm before asking, "How was it to live here during better days? It must have been a wonderful place."

"Yes, Lodz was a delightful town before the war. I had a wonderful childhood with my parents and brothers. We were all so happy back then. I want to be happy again," she said and raised her wonderful brown eyes to look at him.

"I want you to be happy, too," he said, standing up and walking the two steps to her armchair and kneeling beside her.

"Meeting you was...life-changing. And I mean this in more than one way. You saved my honor in Baluty, but you did so much more. Your act of grace restored my belief in man's inherent goodness."

"Anyone would have done the same," Richard said, his cheeks flaming with the praise.

"Nobody else did, and I can't even blame them," she said with a sigh. "Last summer, Jarek and Stan still lived here, but since they went into hiding...I honestly had no idea how to run the farm on my own after the winter. And then you came along," a heart-warming smile lit up her face as she continued, "like a knight in shining armor."

"More like a crippled beggar," Richard said with a sarcastic chuckle. "If I remember right, I had to be carried all the way to your house."

"True. When I saw you there, chained to your friends, I couldn't let them hang you." Tears welled in her eyes and he pressed a quick kiss on her hair. "Anyhow, I'm grateful you're here, cousin Ryszard Blach. It's good to have a man in the house."

Oh, how he would love to be the man of the house. Her man.

He took her hands into his. "One might argue about this, but I consider myself the luckiest man on earth. Because I have found you, Katrina Zdanek." Then he showered her with kisses. Needy, frantic, desperate. He longed to feel her close to him, to show her how much he loved her.

She clung to him, knowing that neither of them might survive the upcoming adventure. But in this very moment nothing mattered beyond their embrace. Tonight they needed to give in to their love for each other.

Richard scooped her up into his arms and carried her upstairs into her room with the big bed that had no doubt belonged to her parents and grandparents before. With the innocence of the first time, they discovered joy and passion in each other's arms.

# CHAPTER 19

Several days later, a visitor arrived at the farmhouse. Out of habit, Richard disappeared from sight and went to work in the shed. He had barely opened the toolbox when Katrina called out for him to join her in the kitchen.

A woman in her fifties sat at the wooden table with a mug of herbal brew in her hands, gray hair tied into a bun at the nape of her neck. She smiled at him and extended her beefy hand with long fingers. "Hello, I'm Magda Lenska, the midwife."

"It's a pleasure to meet you."

"I have a message from your relative. Take a seat." Magda didn't beat around the bush.

The tension in the room ratcheted up as Richard obeyed her request and sat on the chair to her right, facing Katrina on the opposite side of the table. Katrina had told him that the midwife had helped deliver all of the Zdanek siblings, as she had most of the children around Lodz for the past thirty years.

"Your sister-in-law refused to escape," Magda said.

Richard's jaw dropped to the floor. Why would anyone pass up the chance to leave the Ghetto? From all he'd heard, it lingered at the edge of hell on earth. Eighty thousand crammed into a space where formerly twenty thousand had lived, long hours working dangerous and backbreaking jobs in the factories, and little to no food. Above all hovered the constant threat of deportation.

Magda glanced around the big open kitchen as if to make sure nobody was within earshot and lowered her voice to a whisper, "She's hiding your nephew Janusz."

"Janusz is alive? Piotr's son? But how?" Katrina gasped and tears of joy began to flow. "He was deported to Chelmno a year and a half ago. We received communication that all children below the age of twelve were deported." Katrina's voice and hands were trembling like leaves in the wind. "His name was on the list. It was there. Yes, it was." She broke out into sobs.

"It was a horrible day. I was there when Chaim Rumkowski, the head of the Council of Elders, brought perpetual heartbreak over the Ghetto, with his shameful speech." The midwife's eyes glazed over with grief and despair.

"What speech?" Richard hissed.

Magda Lenska looked at him with the eyes of a centenarian, before she stood, her arms stretched wide to her sides. "On German instructions, he made a speech pleading with the inhabitants of the ghetto to give up children ten years of age and younger, so that others might survive. I was there, it was pitiful. Parents screaming, mothers weeping, children howling. I remember every single word of his speech:

"'A grievous blow has struck the ghetto,' he said. 'The Germans are asking us to give up the best we possess: the children and the elderly. I was unworthy of having a child of my own, so I gave the best years of my life to children. I've lived and breathed with children; I never imagined I would be forced to deliver this sacrifice to the altar with my own hands. In my old age, I must stretch out my hands and beg. Brothers and sisters! Hand them over to me! Fathers and mothers – give me your children!'"

After her dramatic recounting, Magda sunk onto the chair, exhausted, overwhelmed. She sobbed quietly for a few minutes, then the midwife raised her head and gazed at them, the sorrow of an entire city reflected in her pained eyes. "Your relative, Agnieska, wouldn't do it. Since then she's been hiding Janusz and sharing her meager rations with him. If she escapes he'll starve within days. That is why she has refused to leave."

"It's all too awful to comprehend," Katrina said.

"God has not left Poland. Miracles do happen, even under Nazi occupation. Your nephew is alive."

"God bless you, Magda. This is the happiest news I have received in years," Katrina said.

"It may not be as happy as you think, my girl," Magda responded. "Stan hinted that you had planned for this man," she nodded at Richard, "to enter the Ghetto in his Wehrmacht uniform and escort Agnieska out with a work permit. This will not happen with a child in tow. I'm sorry I can't be of further help. Thanks for the infusion." The midwife gathered her things to leave.

"We are very grateful for everything you did." Katrina held Magda's hands and kissed them in a gesture of appreciation.

When the midwife left, Richard and Katrina fell into each other's arms, happiness and sorrow fighting for dominance.

Sorrow won.

"What are we to do?" Katrina asked with a feeble voice.

"We'll think of something, my sweetheart." Richard buried his face in the top of her hair and breathed its sweetness as he held his beloved close. He doubted there would be a way to rescue both Agnieska and Janusz, but he knew better than to tell Katrina right now.

"Why is this insanity happening? Why? What have we done to deserve this?" she cried.

"Nothing, my love. Nothing. Sometimes bad things happen to good people."

"How can God allow this?"

# CHAPTER 20

After dusk Stan snuck into the house.
"Thank God, you're here!" Katrina threw her arms around him with such force they both stumbled.

"Calm down, sister, and tell me what happened. I saw the midwife visit with you," Stan said, ignoring Richard's presence.

"She brought good and bad news. Which one do you want to hear first?" Katrina dragged her brother into the kitchen. She and Richard had just finished working on the fields for the day and settled in to have dinner. Wordlessly, Richard put another setting for Stan on the table.

"The bad, please." Richard liked his thinking. Getting it over with and ending on a positive note. In different circumstances they might have been friends.

"Agnieska refused to escape," Katrina said, dishing out *Bigos,* a popular Polish stew made of finely chopped meat, sauerkraut, and shredded fresh white cabbage. The vinegary smell filled the kitchen and made Richard's mouth water. As farmers they had more food at their disposal than most people, but since Katrina helped feed Stan's resistance group, they always scraped by, and she often used her ingenuity to prepare meals with less than common ingredients.

"Why would the stupid woman do this?" Stan asked and chugged down a glass of water.

"Because she's hiding Janusz."

Stan dropped the spoon of *Bigos* about to enter his mouth into the bowl. "What? Little Jan? As in our nephew Jan?"

"Yes." Katrina beamed with joy.

Richard opted not to enter the conversation to prevent rousing Stan's temper, and silently spooned the meal into his mouth. It tasted different, tarter than usual. Then he remembered and grinned, waiting for Stan's reaction.

"Spill it," Stan said to Katrina and took a big bite of stew. His face turned into a grimace. "What the hell have you put in there?"

"Fox." She shrugged.

"God, Katrina. Really? Why not cook a rabbit or a bird?" Stan groaned.

"I cook what I have and Richard happened to bring me a fox. He caught him trying to stalk our hens. The fur will make a nice muff. Now do you want to hear about Jan and Agnieska or not?"

Stan nodded, but first he shot a dark stare at Richard, murmuring, "Thanks for the meat."

She repeated the news they'd received from the midwife and then presented the problem by asking, "How do we get both of them out?"

"Hmm...since Jan is officially not there, we can't get a

pass for him. But this also means nobody will miss him if he disappears," Stan said.

"He can't just climb the fence and run away or he'd have done that a long time ago," Richard said, serving himself seconds of stew. Fox or no fox, this wasn't the time for qualms, and it actually didn't taste that bad once he'd gotten accustomed to the tart flavor.

"Well observed, Fritz. And that would be why? Let me tell you: because your fucking compatriots are shooting everyone who so much as glances the wrong way."

"Please don't start that again, dear brother," Katrina begged. "We have an impossible task ahead and we have to work together or we'd better not try it at all."

Stan gave an indecipherable growl. Katrina obviously knew her brother well, because she smiled and continued to talk, "Magda won't be able to help any further. She's already exposed herself by delivering the messages. If someone found out and betrayed her, it would endanger her entire family."

"Who would betray her except for the..." Stan cast a dirty stare at Richard. "...None of us, right?"

Annoyance snaked up Richard's spine at being the constant subject of Stan's hatred. Wasn't his willingness to expose himself and go inside the Ghetto proof enough of his loyalty? "Look, *Polacke*, there's plenty of collaborators amongst *your* compatriots, willing to sell their souls and betray their own mother for a scrap of bread."

"Could you stop bickering like ten-year-olds for once? Or I'll have to ask Tadzio for help with this. He's more grown up than both of you together." Katrina stood and put her fists on her hips.

"Truce," Stan offered.

"Truce," Richard agreed. But neither of them would go as far as shaking the other's hand.

Katrina returned with paper and pencil. "So what do we know about the Ghetto?"

They talked, planned, designed, scribbled, and drew for hours, but in the end had to accept that there wasn't a way to rescue both of their relatives.

"Let's face it. It's impossible." Stan got up and put on his boots and smock. "I'll return to my unit and see what advice they can give me. Perhaps they know more than we do."

"Yes, talk to Bartosz, he might come up with a plan." Katrina kissed her brother on the cheek. "Be careful and return soon to let me know." Then she stared after him as he disappeared into the night.

"Let's go to bed," Richard said, putting his arm around her shoulders.

Suddenly she seemed so frail, weak even, as she leaned against him and sighed. "I wish we could do something. Anything."

In that very instant Richard promised himself not to let her down. Somehow, he would find a way to rescue her loved ones. It might even help to alleviate the burden of guilt weighing on his shoulders.

* * *

The next day, a Sunday, a neighbor came over and found them working in the backyard.

"Good morning, Katrina," the woman greeted her, "and who's that handsome man living with you? A boyfriend?"

"No, Mrs. Kozlow. This is Ryszard Blach, a distant cousin from up North. He lost his home." Katrina introduced them and Mrs. Kozlow gave Richard a flirtatious smile. He politely shook her hand, trying his best to keep a straight face. Even if he weren't madly in love with Katrina, he wouldn't acknowledge the advances of a woman who was old enough to be his mother.

"May I borrow your heavy shears?" Mrs. Kozlow said. "I need to trim the branches close to the house. Don't want them snapping off and breaking my windows."

"Of course you may. It must be done before summer," Katrina said.

"You are lucky. You have this strong man in your house to help," the woman said slyly. "With my husband dead and my son forced to work in the Reich, my four daughters and I do what we can."

"Forgive me, I didn't mean to be thoughtless," Katrina replied. "I will send Ryszard over to you if you need any heavy work done."

Richard didn't like the way Mrs. Kozlow's eyes brightened at Katrina's offer, but in order not to give his German accent away, he remained silent and only gave a curt nod.

"My daughters would love the company of your cousin, I'm sure of that. There's little enough diversion in our lives. Work, and more work. Day in and day out," the woman complained.

"I thought you weren't allowed to work anymore?" Katrina said, and turned to Richard to explain. "Mrs. Kozlow is a teacher, but the Germans have closed down the secondary school where she used to work."

Richard nodded. In Hitler's racial theories, the Slavs

130

were at the bottom of the pyramid, slightly above the Jews. Considered an inferior race, they weren't deemed worthy of receiving a higher education, and thus all secondary schools for Poles had been closed down, making thousands of teachers redundant.

"Thanks to an acquaintance, I found work in the children's camp."

"I've never heard of a children's camp. Where's this?" Katrina asked.

Her neighbor laughed before saying, "That's because you're always out here on the farm and never venture into town. The children's camp, or *Kinder KZ*, as the Germans call it, is attached to the Ghetto, separated by a fence. It's a prison for underage criminals."

"And you're teaching there?"

"No, silly, of course not. The little criminals have to work. I'm there to oversee that they behave. It's not a satisfying job," she wrinkled her nose before continuing, "but the pay is excellent and includes extra rations. What more could I want?"

*Decency and morale perhaps.* Richard had never been in the Kinder KZ, but he'd heard stories about it. The living conditions in there mirrored those of concentration camps for adults. He couldn't fathom how a woman, a mother, and a Pole could voluntarily work there. For all he knew the children never left the camp again, except for those destined for Germanization. Polish Christian youngsters with Nordic ethnic features would be selected by racial officers and brought to a transit camp before being sent to the Reich for adoption by racially pure German parents.

# CHAPTER 21

"What's troubling you, my love?" Richard asked, putting his arm around Katrina's shoulders.

"Nothing." She pushed him away, pretending to be busy tending to the bunnies.

"I can see that you're worried, since you have that frown on your forehead," Richard said, trying to sound carefree. The uncertainty about the fates of her family had taken a toll on Katrina and she was closing herself down, shutting him out. Like a fish, she seemed to slip from his hands whenever he tightened his grip. Since he adored her with all his heart and soul, the prospect of losing her caused his entire body to constrict with grief.

"Things are such a mess," she finally said. "For all the rumors of an end to the war, nothing has changed. Deportations from the Ghetto can start any day now and we still haven't the slightest clue how to rescue Agnieska and Jan…" She wiped a strand of hair from her face and left a dirty smear in its place.

Richard instinctively raised his hand to swipe it away, but stopped midair. Given the way she'd recently reacted to his signs of affection, it would probably only heighten the tension. Since the day Stan had left to find out more about the Ghetto, Katrina's strength and determination seemed to have gone with him, and an empty shell of her former self remained. It pained Richard to see her like this, but she stubbornly refused to let him share her burden. If Katrina suffered, he ached right along with her.

"My darling, you mustn't give up," Richard said. "I'm sure Stan will return any moment with a plan."

"He'd better hurry. The Germans had another of their roundups yesterday, detaining everyone caught in the net," Katrina said bitterly and put the rabbit into the open enclosure with grass. "All males above the age of fifteen without a sealed and stamped *Arbeitskarte* were sent to work for the Reich." Every Pole had to register with the General Government and was issued a work card. Those without a job were always at risk of being caught in one of the roundups and sent to Germany as forced laborers.

"I'm sorry…" There wasn't much else he could say.

Katrina turned around and her brown eyes glinted sparks of anger at him. "You are sorry! That's all you can say? My parents are dead. Murdered by German soldiers. Ludmila and Jarek are dead, also at the hands of your kind. Piotr is probably dead. Agnieska and Jan will soon be dead, too! Stan is all that is left of my family and God knows for how long." More tears streamed down her cheeks with every word tumbling from her mouth.

"Please, calm down." Despite knowing better, Richard reached out for her.

"Don't you dare touch me! You're one of them bloody Germans!" She yelled at the top of her lungs, sending the rabbits in the enclosure in a frenzy to find cover.

He couldn't deny the truth of her careless words. He was the enemy. His nation had brought so much death and destruction to Poland and its people, Katrina had every right to be angry with him. He'd deluded himself into thinking that their love could conquer all barriers. Love alone wasn't enough. Not in these troubled times – times painted with the dark and destructive brush of war and death.

"Stan is clever. He'll stay safe and return soon," Richard said, hoping the reassurance would somehow calm her down. It didn't. She smothered him with curses, until violent sobs racked her body and forced the fight out of her. Katrina dropped to the floor, a pale, cold, blubbering picture of misery.

And he'd caused it.

"Katrina, darling, are you alright?" Richard asked, the fear seeping into his bones. But she wouldn't answer. Incoherent scraps of words in Polish and German, mixed with sobs, bubbled out of her mouth. *Frontkoller*. He'd witnessed the meltdown of comrades at the front, caving in to the physical and mental pressures there. He'd just never thought this could happen in the rural idyll of a farmhouse.

There and then, Richard realized the burden placed on her delicate shoulders: single-handedly managing the farm, worrying about her insurgent brothers, feeding a group of partisans, and sheltering a *German* fugitive had been too overwhelming to withstand.

Her resilience had been used up. With his heart shattered into a million pieces, Richard knew he must do the right thing – lessen her burden. He scooped her up, and carried her upstairs to her bedroom. He tucked her in, soothed her to sleep, and pressed a kiss to her chilly forehead.

Downstairs in the kitchen he sat down to write a letter.

*Beloved Katrina,*

*My presence here is putting too much of a burden on your shoulders and it endangers not only you, but also those you support. Thus, I must leave. I do so with a broken heart, because my love for you will never vanish. My hope is to see you again in more benign circumstances.*

*I pray you survive this terrible time and find your family. I have never been, nor ever will be, an enemy to you and yours.*

*Wishing you nothing but happiness.*

*Always your Richard.*

*PS: Please give my greetings to Tadzio and your brother.*

He retrieved his uniform from its hiding place and put it on beneath his peasant clothes, before packing a bag with his meager belongings, stuffing some bread and a bottle of water inside as well.

Then he returned upstairs and leaned against the door-jamb, gazing one last time at Katrina's dear face framed by the long hair he so loved.

As a violent ache ripped through his chest, he left.

# CHAPTER 22

Richard had nowhere to go. He couldn't very well return to his unit after being AWOL for so many weeks. The memory of the interrogation in Warsaw was still vivid, and they wouldn't give him the benefit of doubt the second time around. Having to face a firing squad wasn't on his list of things to do, so returning to Wehrmacht barracks was out of the question.

Tadzio's house came to mind, but Richard had left Katrina to protect her and her family, so how could he impose the threat of his existence on his only friend Tadzio now? No. Richard shook his head. He had to steer clear of anyone he knew and loved.

He walked along the road leading to Lodz, pondering his options. There weren't many left. Hiding in the woods might be one. But the dense forest around Lodz was infested with partisans and Jews in hiding, hardly a place where a German would be welcomed with open arms.

If his own compatriots didn't kill him first, the Polish

resistance would. A grim smile appeared on his face as he thought about the satisfaction Stan would feel at the notice of Richard's demise. At least one person would be happy then.

Richard trudged forward, the church tower of Lodz appearing in the distance. If only he knew what to do. Where to go. He sat down on a rock alongside the road, taking a long gulp from his water bottle. Leaving Katrina had destroyed his spirits and shattered his heart. Unable to find a silver lining, he flopped onto his back, looking up into the sky, where white fair-weather clouds chased each other. They formed peculiar shapes, two clouds coalescing into a tank, cupola, barrel, and muzzle. It obscured the sun for a while, before the wind tore it apart again, two rabbits nibbling a carrot between them.

Then one of the rabbits changed form again, transmuting into his sister Lotte's face.

"You're giving up? Really? I never had you down for a quitter," she taunted him. His ears rang with her sermon, as if she stood at his side bristling with righteous anger the way she had so many times during their childhood. "People are about to die and you're wrapped up in self-pity? Miserable coward!"

"What do you know about life, Lotte? I'm not a coward."

"Prove it. Get your ass up and save that boy and his aunt." The cloud metamorphosed again into an overdimensioned fist. Richard broke out into laughter. His youngest sister would haunt him even in the afterlife, should he fail his mission. For all he knew she might be there already. The negative thought sobered him.

"I'll rescue Jan and Agnieska, alright? If only to prove

that I'm not a lousy coward. And you'd better be alive when I get home, sister."

A million ideas flooded his mind as he tried to come up with a plan. He was too absorbed in his thoughts to notice a group of men who suddenly surrounded him.

"Who are you, stranger, and what are you doing here?" a filthy-looking man asked with a rifle at the ready. Being held at gunpoint seemed to have become an annoying habit.

"My name is Ryszard Blach," he said in the drawl he'd practiced with Katrina to disguise his German accent. "I'm from up North, displaced by the Soviets first, and by the Germans second. I came all the way here to stay with my relatives, but I lost my way."

"What might be the name of your relatives?" one man asked shrewdly.

"Lenska," Richard responded, cold sweat running down his back, "Magda Lenska is my second cousin once removed."

"Ah, Magda Lenska, the midwife. She's a good woman." The haggard and filthy man eyed Richard and the pack slung over his shoulder. "One of my men can take you there right now, but it's a considerable deviation from our ways and quite dangerous."

Richard understood and opened his pack. "Take this as a reward for your generous offer," he said, holding out the bread and cheese to the leader of the group. He could all but see the saliva as the hungry men's mouths watered, while their eyes remained glued on the food.

Minutes later, not a morsel of bread remaining, the leader of the group said, "Zych will bring you to your cousin."

Zych obviously was a code name, because the mentioned man – or rather boy – needed a moment to process the request and nod. Richard hid a grin. Soldier Zych was a character in a historical novel of the Polish Nobel laureate Henryk Sienkiewicz. Richard had devoured all of his books that had been translated into German, most notably the novel *Quo Vadis*, about the persecution of Christians under Emperor Nero. The boy did show a sense of irony in choosing his nom de guerre.

"Thank you," Richard said and followed the boy through the woods. After about four hours of vigorous walking over rough and smooth terrain, circling around Lodz instead of taking the short – German-guarded – main road, Zych stopped and pointed at a building slightly higher than the others. "See this house? Turn to the left until you pass a haberdashery, then it's the second house on the right side. Good luck."

Richard turned to thank the boy, who couldn't be much older than fourteen, but he'd already drifted away into the protective shield of the trees. His palms sweaty despite the chilly early summer night, Richard set out to follow the boy's directions to Magda Lenska's house, as a troubling thought came to his mind. *Curfew.*

This time of year the nights were short. He couldn't risk violating curfew without the protection of darkness. And he sure as hell didn't want to run into the Blue Police, the auxiliary police manned by Poles or Polish-speaking Ukrainians, or worse, into one of his former comrades. So he settled against a tree, waiting for dawn to arrive. At daybreak he ventured into Lodz to find Magda Lenska's house.

If she was surprised to find him knocking at her door, she kept her expression neutral and invited him inside.

# CHAPTER 23

Richard sat in the midwife's small but cozy salon, a cup of herb tea in his hand. The salon was equipped with a couch, a small coffee table, and two chairs. The furniture was old, but well kept. The walls were beautifully adorned with pictures of mothers and their newborns, scribbled notes of thanks, and paintings of Lodz.

"Please call me Magda, everyone else does," she said, sitting on the couch opposite to him. She had the rare gift of making anyone around her feel at ease, welcome, and appreciated.

"Thank you, Magda. I appreciate your kindness." He glanced at her, hoping it had been the right decision to come here. She wouldn't betray him – he hoped. But he didn't want to cause her problems either.

"So what brings you here?" she asked, eyeing him with curiosity.

Richard gave a deep sigh, avoiding her scrutinizing glance. "It is…we…we couldn't come up with a plan. We thought about a hundred different ways, but none would work. We can either save the boy or his aunt, but both of them, next to impossible." He rubbed his scruff. One night out in the woods and he probably looked as dirty as he felt. "Sorry for my appearance. I arrived after curfew last night."

"Oh, that darn curfew." Angry glints lit up her eyes as she continued, "Those Germans seem to think that babies adhere to a schedule and are born only during office hours. Since the wife of a high-ranking Nazi almost died during delivery, because I was delayed by a patrol, I have a special pass to go about my work after curfew. But the people coming for my help don't. We'll all be so much happier when they're finally gone."

A slight shiver raked down his spine. Despite the midwife's kindness, she obviously hated the German occupiers as much as the next person did. And that included him.

"I'm afraid I can't help you with your endeavor. As I already said, I can smuggle messages in and out of the Ghetto, but not much more," Magda said, sipping the tea. "Why are you really here?"

Shame crossed Richard's face as he remembered Katrina's outburst. "We had a row, Katrina and I, and I thought it best to leave. It's safer for her. My presence at the farm will sooner or later cause unwanted enquiries."

Magda, like many Poles living in this region, had grown up bilingual and she effortlessly switched from Polish to German, "…because despite your peasant garb and fluent Polish you're not really a cousin from up North. I've been there, and the accent is distinct from yours." It didn't make sense to lie to her, not if he wanted to enlist her help.

"I believe you already guessed it. I'm one of the abhorred Germans. A Wehrmacht soldier. A deserter. A man wanted on both sides. When I left Katrina, I realized I had nowhere to go, nowhere to hide. Partisans picked me up and the only name that came to my mind was yours. Please forgive me for endangering you. I should leave," he said, tired, and put his cup on the coffee table.

"Don't," Magda said, putting a hand on his arm. "My job is to bring life into this world. How could I risk yours by sending you away? Eat some and then sleep. We'll talk in the evening."

Richard nodded and ate the *Pierogi*, vegetable-filled dumplings she put in front of him. Then he settled to sleep in the corner of the room, while Magda left to visit her clients. When she returned in the evening, Richard felt as if born again. A sound six hours of shut-eye, food, and a wash and shave had worked wonders not only on his looks but also on his mood.

The row with Katrina remained weighing heavy on his mind. As much as he believed his leaving to be for the best, he hated the way they had parted. Magda must have picked up on his sadness, because she said, "You should return to the farm. I know love when I see it, and you and Katrina Zdanek are clearly in love."

"It's for the best. She'll be better off without me," Richard insisted.

"There's so little affection in the world these days and life itself is so tenuous. Love should be held tightly and treasured. It's what keeps us going when the world seems bleak. It fills our hearts with hope and our souls with courage to fight on when defeat seems inevitable. Only love can move mountains and make miracles happen. I experience this every day in my work."

"She doesn't want me anymore."

"My son, when you grow as old as I am you'll discover the error of your ways. This girl is young and confused. She bears the burden of so many losses on her shoulders and still helps those prepared to fight for our country, God bless her. But it's taking a toll on her and it's only natural to blame you for all she has suffered at the hands of Germans in time of great distress. Put yourself in her place, and if you love her as you say, help her walk through her ordeal of loss instead of running away like coward. Be a man; be the bigger person and go back to her. I know she will welcome you with open arms."

"I'm not..." Richard balled his hands into fists. ...*a coward*. Or was he? Maybe leaving turned him into a greater coward than staying. "I can't return until I've proven my loyalty to her. And I intend to do that by rescuing Janusz and Agnieska. I must do this to gain Katrina's respect. Her brother Stan despises me and I would like to earn his respect, too. I would like to be treated as a friend instead of a fiendish foe."

"I can see you are a gentle soul," the midwife replied. "I, too, would much rather save a life than destroy it. I will help you, and I pray your efforts are successful. Let's go to the kitchen and make *Pierogi*; cooking always helps me to relax my mind." Richard followed her into the kitchen and watched her work, while they chatted of this and that, trying to come up with ideas how to save Katrina's family.

Richard noticed her medical bag standing by the front door, always ready in case a woman in labor needed urgent assistance. Beside it hung her overcoat and a hat. Magda washed her hands after kneading the dough. An annoying trickle penetrated his mind and he glanced around to find the source of the noise. A dripping faucet.

"It's been dripping for weeks," Magda said with a shrug.

"May I try to fix it?" he asked.

"Feel free. There's a toolbox beneath the sink."

Richard found the toolbox and started working on the faucet. At least he could be of some help to the woman who'd so generously received him in her house. Once done with the faucet, he dedicated his attention to a rickety shelf. It was obvious that there was no man in the house.

"What about your family?" he asked, glancing around for more things needing repair.

"My four children are all grown up, living with their own families. And my husband has been forced to work in the Reich. Haven't heard from him in a while..." She shrugged, apparently trying to make the nostalgia go away. "I'm usually too busy to worry. You'd think that during war, fewer children are born, but no. It's quite the opposite."

The word *children* caused the wheels in his brain to turn. "What do you know about the Kinder KZ?" Richard asked.

"I've never been there myself, although it's separated from the Ghetto only by a wooden fence. Why do you ask?"

"Recently, a neighbor, Mrs. Kozlow, came to borrow the farm's heavy shears and she works in the Kinder KZ."

"Tekla Koszlow?" Magda grimaced. "I know her well, since I delivered her five babies. The woman doesn't have an ounce of integrity or compassion in her body. All she cares about are her own interests. I can just imagine how she enjoys working there."

Richard had gotten the same impression when he'd first met Mrs. Koszlow a few days ago, but chose not to discuss her character traits, "Mrs. Kozlow mentioned that the camp isn't well guarded. Not like the Ghetto or the camps for adults."

"Go on," the midwife encouraged him, as she formed the dough into crescent-shaped pieces.

"If Janusz can sneak into the children's camp–"

"He'd jump out of the frying pan and into the fire," Magda interrupted him, stuffing the dough pieces with herbs and mashed potatoes.

"I have heard that children with Nordic features are selected for Germanization and sent to adoption into the Reich. Perhaps Janusz…"

"Little Jan?" The midwife laughed. "He has the high cheekbones and dark eyes of his mother, a beautiful woman by the way. He looks like a poster child for the Slav race. That is when I saw him last about four years ago. Furthermore, his presence there would cause ten kinds of questions. You as a German should know how meticulous your countrymen are keeping lists of everything," Magda said, expertly folding the dough into the dumplings called *Pierogi*.

Richard felt his spirits sink and momentarily he doubted his fitness to shoulder the huge responsibility he had taken on. He hadn't thought about that part. Even if they took Janusz for Germanization they'd soon start asking questions about his origin. It wouldn't take long until someone recognized him. For a while Richard watched Magda working in silence as she boiled water on the range.

"So if he's not on any of their lists, nobody will notice when he goes missing, right?" Richard thought out loud.

Magda nodded.

"You said the Kinder KZ is separated from the Ghetto by a flimsy wooden fence. If he can somehow sneak into the camp at night, then early in the morning I can go there, posing as an official from the Racial Institute, pick out Janusz, and leave with him."

"You? In that peasant garb? They'd shoot you before you had a chance to utter a single word." Magda put the dumplings into the boiling water. "Dinner is almost ready. Would you help me set the table please?"

Richard nodded, and carried the dishes over to the small kitchen table. "I still have my uniform. I've been hiding it in the woods before coming to your house."

"More astute than I've given you credit for," she said with a smile. "Of course with your Wehrmacht uniform it might just work. The sentries are Polish and they probably won't dare question you."

Richard's brain raced a mile a minute, searching for a viable rescue option, while he stuffed *Pierogi* into his mouth. "Those are delicious; best I've ever eaten," he said.

"It's a recipe handed down for generations in my family." Magda beamed with pride and ate a piece herself. "There's just one problem. How will you even find Jan?"

"Uhmmm…I haven't considered that," he said. According to Mrs. Koszlow, at any given time close to two thousand children lived and worked in the camp. Looking for one boy would be like looking for the proverbial needle in a haystack. Even if Richard knew the boy. Which he didn't.

How would he be able to pick out a boy he'd never seen? For a fleeting moment he considered asking Katrina to accompany him, but that would only make the mission more complicated and endanger her. No, he had the best chance for success if he did this alone.

"What if…" Richard ran his hands through his hair and shot a glance toward the midwife. "…Please hear me out first, before you decide. What if you delivered another message to Agnieska, letting her know the exact time and place where Janusz has to wait for me to pick him up?"

"We'd need detailed information about the children's camp. Information from the inside," Magda said and they both looked at each other before they spoke at once: "Tekla Koszlow."

"It looks like I have to visit with her tomorrow. You lie low and think about the plan. There's so much to prepare to ensure it works. Also, you still want to rescue Agnieska."

Richard paled; in his excitement over the children's camp, he'd all but forgotten about her.

\* \* \*

The next day, pins and needles of anxious energy prickled his skin as he waited for Magda to return from her social visit with Mrs. Koszlow.

"How did it go?" he asked the moment Magda closed the door behind her.

"Well, very well indeed. Let's sit at the table," she answered. On the way to the table, she grabbed a pencil and piece of paper. "Tekla was so busy showing off her important work with the Germans, she never noticed I was quizzing her."

Richard watched with excitement as she drew a pretty

accurate map of the Ghetto and the Kinder KZ, including the factories and the sleeping barracks.

"Here." Richard pointed at a rectangle behind the other barracks, but close to the gate. "What's this?"

"The quarantine barracks for the seriously ill. Tekla said nobody likes to go there, fearful of contracting a disease."

"That's the perfect meeting place, then." Richard beamed. "If Janusz could hide around there, I'll surely find him right away."

"Good idea." Magda nodded and finished her map, putting a door into the fence separating the Ghetto from the children's camp. "Here, this gate." She tapped her finger on the map. "This might solve our problem on how to rescue Agnieska."

Richard looked at her, not quite understanding. The midwife grinned at him, saying, "Loose-lipped Tekla provided me with plenty of invaluable information."

CHAPTER 24

The next days passed in a blur of activity. Richard and Magda perfected their plan, going through everything several times. On paper it looked good, but he knew it was flimsy at best. Yet it was all they had. And they couldn't wait, as indications for the beginning of final deportation and closure of the Ghetto were becoming more evident by the day.

Magda delivered the message to Agnieska with precise instructions for Jan to climb across the fence under the cover of night and to hide near the quarantine barracks until Richard picked him up.

Richard had retrieved his Wehrmacht uniform from the woods, and produced an ID card that looked similar enough to the real thing to fool an uninterested Polish sentry.

Agnieska had arranged to be assigned to teach new camp children how to assemble baskets for artillery ammunition for the German war machine. Since the Germans didn't do their dirty work themselves, they left this task to the Jews.

"It's now or never," Richard said one day.

"Tomorrow is the day," Magda said, winking, "just one more thing to do." Then she put on her coat and grabbed her medical bag.

"Good luck," Richard said. This part of the plan was crucial to rescue not only Jan but also his aunt. At the same time it was the most difficult task to prepare. So many things could go wrong. If Tekla became suspicious, it might even endanger the entire mission.

Richard could barely sit and paced the room not once, but at least a hundred times. He tried busying his hands with writing letters – one to his family, another one to Katrina. In case he died, Magda would see that they arrived at their recipients. But he hoped to tell Katrina in person how much he loved her. And his family soon thereafter, once the war ended.

When Magda returned several hours later, he barely hid his trembling hands.

"Poor Tekla, she got sick." The midwife smirked and Richard wanted to cry with relief.

"Thank God, it worked," he uttered. Magda had laced donut-like *Paczki* with special herbs and offered them to Tekla. Just as she had predicted, the greedy woman had gobbled up all of them, leaving only one for Magda, and within the hour she was running relays to the outhouse in the backyard.

"In her panic over losing her prestigious job with the Germans, she begged me for help," Magda reported. "I gave her a dose of medicine that'll knock her out for twenty-four hours and promised to arrange for a substitute to fill in for her for the day." Magda waved the special permit issued for those who worked in the children's camp.

Richard swallowed hard. Their narrow window of opportunity had opened briefly. It would last for one day, or else... He didn't shut his eyes all night, his mind circling around the plan and everything that might go wrong. There was no Plan B in place and only with God's help would all four of them still be alive next week.

Early in the morning he shaved and put on his uniform, washed and meticulously ironed by Magda. Breakfast didn't appeal to him, since his stomach did somersaults in apprehension of things to come.

"Good luck," Magda said, pulling him into a hug. "Remember to always keep calm. Even if things go awry, don't lose your gait and never flinch or run."

*If I do, I'll get shot in the back.*

He nodded. In theory he knew all that. During his days in the security division he'd learned how to single out a guilty suspect. It always came back to showing nerves. Only the innocent – or the wicked – stayed relatively calm despite fear.

But being on the other side was a lot more nerve-wracking than he'd believed it would be. Palms sweating, he snuck out of Magda's place before dawn and lingered in the shadows until it was time to approach the Kinder KZ at seven o'clock sharp.

*Please, God, let everything work out.* Richard had memorized the inside of the camp from Magda's map, but he could only hope Mrs. Koszlow had given an accurate report.

He approached the gate, noticing the sentry in the glass

case, unarmed. Apparently, nobody expected the children to try and escape. Richard took one last calming breath and stepped in front of the tiny window, showing his fake ID card and barking at the sentry, "Klausen. Racial Institute."

The sentry took one glance at Richard's field gray uniform, complete with field cap, and opened the gate for him.

His heart thundering in his throat, Richard marched across the assembly space, taking inventory out of the corner of his eye. The alignment of the barracks resembled more or less the rectangles on the map, and he turned left toward where the quarantine barracks were supposed to be.

A deep sigh escaped him, when he saw the stone building, even more rickety than the rest. He moved out of sight of the gate and behind the building, expecting to find Jan and Agnieska waiting for him there.

Nothing.

Richard almost screamed with disappointment, when he remembered that Jan would be hiding until he whistled "W żłobie leży," a popular Polish Christmas carol. He hadn't finished the first verse of the melody when a horribly emaciated boy crawled out from his hiding.

"Janusz Zdanek?"

The boy nodded.

"Where's your aunt?"

"In…in…the factory…I suppose. She said to leave her things here, for when she finds a way to sneak out."

Richard removed Mrs. Koszlow's uniform and employee card from under his smock and hid it beneath a bush. Then he scrutinized the boy's clothing. It was shabby, but that was normal in war-ridden Poland. At least Agnieska had thought to remove the blue star on a white background from Jan's shirt. Richard smiled and again addressed the boy, who'd been watching him with eyes wide open. "I'm going to bring you to your family, but you have to act terrified of me. Can you do this?"

Jan nodded. Apparently seeing the Wehrmacht uniform terrorized him so much already he didn't have to fake his angst.

Richard grabbed his arm tighter and dragged the boy behind, just like any soldier would with a criminal boy. As they reached the exit, Richard expected the sentry to show the same disinterest as before and open the gate for the German soldier without a question.

"Hey! Where are you going with that boy?" the sentry asked as he left his glass case.

"Herr...Dymek," Richard read from the sentry's lapel, "is that the respectful way you address an official from the Racial Institute? I might have to give word to your superior."

The man didn't budge and Richard summoned all his strength to glower at him, whilst grabbing Jan's arm tighter, afraid he might make a dash for freedom. "For your information, the Commandant himself wants this boy to be sent for Germanization and I am taking him to the transit camp."

"I haven't seen you here before," the sentry argued.

"What's your point, Polacke?" Richard raised his voice for effect but the Pole remained belligerent and wouldn't stamp the fake release papers or open the gate. "You've seen the papers. What else do you want? If you haven't noticed, I have work to do. The truck to transport the children is standing by, waiting for this last passenger."

"Can't authorize every bit of paper that comes to me." The man remained rigid and continued to eye Richard and Jan suspiciously. "Have to read these documents carefully. The Commandant doesn't tolerate mistakes."

"The commandant sure is in a foul mood today, so why don't you walk over to his office and tell him you delayed the transfer. That should cheer him up, right?" Richard sensed that the man was so close to relenting. Before he could reconsider again, he played his ace in the hole. "I'll tell you what you can do, you insolent fellow! Keep this boy and hand him over to the office yourself. I'll be sure to include your name in my report to the Reichsstatthalter himself. Looks like there's plenty of stubborn Jewish blood running in your veins."

The sentry blanched and in the next moment the seal landed with a mighty thump on the boy's permit. Richard stomped off with Janusz in tow, grumbling at the sentry, who was opening the gate for the impostor in uniform.

The furious Herr Dymek took his sweet time to turn the key and unlock the gate, bringing Richard near to hyperventilating. Why didn't that stupid man hurry up? Of course he knew the answer. It was the small revenge of a powerless Pole, who hated his occupiers as much as the next person, despite working for them.

After what felt like an eternity, the door swung open and Richard pressed out a breath of relief. With superhuman self-control he managed to walk out the gate as if he didn't just steal a Jewish boy destined to be killed from under the Nazi's noses.

But the next splash of cold water wasn't long in coming.

# CHAPTER 25

Richard was dragging the terrorized boy through the gate when he saw two German soldiers approaching the camp, a boy of fifteen or sixteen wedged between them.

"Let me go! I ain't no thief. Didn't steal nothing," the kicking, punching, and struggling boy shouted at the soldiers escorting him. The two men were too busy keeping the little maniac under control to look up. But Richard didn't need to see the face to recognize one of them. How could he not?

The broad shoulders, the authoritative gait, and the low but deep voice belonged unmistakably to his former group leader, Obergefreiter Johann Hauser. Richard's legs twitched, the instinct to take to his heels fighting a fierce battle with rational thought. Somehow, he managed to stay in place, hoping against hope to fake his way out of the situation.

He took a determined step out onto the street, pretending he and Jan weren't on the verge of being shot at point blank range, while he prayed that Johann wouldn't look up, wouldn't recognize him, wouldn't…

Too late.

The second soldier punched the kicking boy and Johann raised his glance to address the sentry, standing three steps behind Richard and Jan. His eyes locked with Richard's for one long, agonizing moment. A moment that extended into two, while time seemed to stand still. The flash of recognition passed across Johann's face, before he tore his eyes off the former friend to the squirming boy he held. An emaciated, filthy boy of eleven years whose body looked the part of an eight-year-old, but whose eyes reflected the immeasurable suffering of the entire Jewish race.

Richard's heart pounded wildly in his chest. *It's over.* Caught red-handed. A supposedly dead German and a Jewish boy. There was nothing to quibble over or interpret.

Johann was a good man with morals, not some vandalizing SS pervert who found joy in looting, raping, and murdering. But he still was a soldier, bound to Hitler's and the Wehrmacht's rules.

Johann's eyes returned to Richard, who formed his lips into a silent plead. A barely noticeable nod was the answer, before Johann raised his right hand to salute. "*Sieg Heil!*"

"*Sieg Heil,*" Richard answered and stepped aside to let Johann's group pass through the gate. Then he told Jan, "Hurry, or we'll be late."

Cold sweat running down his back, Richard hissed like a steam engine as he tried to put on a calm façade. Together they walked down the block and turned at the first corner. He leaned against the building with wobbly legs, his breath coming in spurts. The poor boy seemed equally shaken, even though he couldn't have known how close they had been to disaster.

"Jan," Richard said, crouching down. "How well do you know your way around here?"

"I used to come here with Pa and Ma all the time... before..." Tears started to well in his eyes.

"Can you find your way out of Lodz to your aunt Katrina's farm?"

"Sure. I'm not little anymore, you know?"

Richard had to laugh at Jan's eagerness to be grown up. "I know that. And you have done a fantastic job so far. So listen up, it's important to do exactly as I say, you understand?"

"Yes. Will you now go and rescue Aunt Agni as well?"

"No. I can't go back to the camp or the sentry will get suspicious." Richard stopped talking when Jan's lips began to tremble. "Hey, warrior, remember we left the uniform and ID card of a camp employee for your aunt? She'll simply put it on and walk out of the gate with her head held high." Richard wished it would be that easy. There were a million things that could go wrong, but all he could do was wait. "Now for you and me. It's too dangerous to be seen together. You walk along the main road to the farm and hide in the woods just behind the big field."

"And you?"

"I'll get rid of my uniform and meet you there." Richard paused for a moment before continuing, "If I haven't arrived by dusk...then there's no need to wait for me. You make sure Katrina is alone, then sneak to the back door and knock. She'll let you in."

"You're nice, despite your uniform," Jan said and the compliment warmed Richard's heart.

"Remember your name is Jan Blach and you're from up North, looking for relatives here. But better not to be asked in the first place." He squeezed the boy's hand for a moment and then slapped his butt. "Now go."

Jan trotted off and soon disappeared from Richard's sight. It made sense for them to part ways, but he still itched to go after him and stay by his side – protect him from whatever might come his way.

Richard had stored his peasant clothes beneath a bush on the brink of the woods and hoped they would still be there. The uniform had served its purpose; continuing to wear it would be a liability. He changed into his peasant garb and took the long winding road through the forests back to Katrina's farm, from where he had sallied forth to his endeavor more than a week ago.

His thoughts remained aggrieved, worrying about the safety of Jan, Agnieska, and Magda. A wave of gratefulness poured into his veins when he remembered Johann's small but momentous gesture. He resolved to thank him properly, one day, if both of them survived this ghastly war. Then his thoughts wandered to Katrina. Beautiful, sweet, intelligent, strong, independent Katrina. If only she'd be able to see past his nationality and open her arms for him again. He'd missed her every single minute of the past week, and with every step he took toward her farm, his emotions grew more intense. Several hours of solitary marching through the dusky forest didn't help to calm him down. What if…no, it didn't make sense to dwell on the worst possible outcome. All he could do was to tell her how much he loved her.

Just as he'd been told to, Janusz sat beneath a tree, leaning against the trunk.

"Hey, Jan," Richard called out.

But the boy didn't move. When Richard approached him, he noticed the angelic face with closed eyes and a peaceful smile upon his lips. His throat constricted, but the next moment a relieved chuckle left his mouth as he noticed the boy's chest moving up and down.

He squatted by Jan's side and put a hand on his arm. "Hey, big boy, time to wake up."

Jan opened his eyes in shock, then his mouth. Before he could scream, Richard pressed a big hand over his mouth and said, "Shush. It's me. Richard. Remember, I rescued you from the camp?"

Understanding hit Jan's dark brown eyes and he nodded.

"I'll take my hand away now – promise you won't scream?"

Another nod.

"I wasn't asleep," Jan said with an air of importance. "I merely closed my eyes to better listen to the sound of the forest."

"I know, warrior." Richard nodded with an equally serious expression. "Now let's go and surprise your Aunt Katrina."

Joy and mischief returned to Jan's expression as they walked across the field into the backyard, past the rabbit enclosure, the hen coop, and the herb garden to the back door. Richard inhaled a deep breath, filled with the unique aroma of thyme, lemon balm, and peppermint. It smelled like Katrina. He smiled and knocked on the back door.

She opened and looked at him, the boy, then back at

him, before she broke out into a squeal. "You're back! And you brought my nephew with you!" Then she threw her arms around Jan, raising him into the air and raining kisses on his dear face.

Jan wrinkled his nose with the righteous disgust of an eleven-year-old treated like a child, but soon saw the futility of his silent protest and wrapped his arms around his aunt. Richard discreetly looked the other way when big tears streamed down the boy's cheeks, leaving dirty smears in their path. It was only minutes later when she released the boy and wrapped her arms in a tight embrace around Richard.

"I'm so sorry for my cruel outburst, my darling," she whispered, "Please say you forgive me, or I'll never have a moment's peace again."

"There's nothing to forgive, my love. Terrible things have happened to you and I understand why you lashed out. Please don't think of me as a terrible person. I hope you know me better than that."

"You are the noblest, kindest, most caring person I've ever known. The war tends to make our men hard and bitter like it did to Stan and Jarek. But not you, you've preserved the kindness of your soul." Katrina wept with joy, saying, "I love you, Richard Klausen, and those past days without you were hell. Don't you ever leave my side again."

"I won't." Richard kissed her deep and long, until Jan's giggle caught his attention. The boy made a slightly disgusted grimace, grumbling something similar to "sappy adults."

"You both must be hungry," Katrina said and walked over to the range, fixing a quick meal of leftover boiled potatoes and spinach. When she served each one a plate with a modest-sized portion, Jan's eyes spilled over with disbelief. "That's all for me?"

"All this," Katrina assured him. "And later you can have more."

Jan emptied his plate within seconds, but when Richard wanted to push his plate over to the child, Katrina said, "No. His stomach isn't used to that much food. He has to go slow." She was turning around to pour them water when a flicker of fear crossed her face. "What about Agnieska? In all the excitement, I totally forgot about her."

"We'll have to wait," Richard replied and stood to carry his empty plate to the sink. "If everything goes according to plan, she'll show up here tonight."

Katrina didn't wait for him to finish his sentence before she launched herself into his arms, showering his face with kisses. All the tension left his body like a river flowing toward the ocean. Everything would end well. He was exactly where he wanted to be, with the woman he loved in his embrace. He captured her mouth with his and reveled in her sweet taste, the softness of her lips and tongue, the love and desire coursing through his body.

"Hmm. Hmm," a deep voice harrumphed into Richard's ear.

He broke the kiss and stared directly into Stan's crimson-red face.

# CHAPTER 26

"So, you're back like a bad penny?" Stan growled.

"Stan, shut up for a moment and see who Richard has brought back with him," Katrina scolded her brother as she pointed at Jan.

Stan's jaw fell open and he uttered in disbelief, "Is that you? Jan? Is that really you?"

"Uncle Stan?" Jan answered.

"It's you. Thank God! You're alive!" He took the boy in his arms, kissing him and hugging him so tightly that the boy struggled and ran off to hide behind Katrina.

Stan stood in the middle of the room, turning his cap in his hands, intently studying the toes of his shoes. When he finally raised his head to meet Richard's eyes, his expression was full of shame. "I guess…maybe you're not such a bad guy after all…"

Richard didn't feel schadenfreude at how the other man struggled admitting his mistake. He probably would have reacted the same way, if one of his sisters – God forbid –

had fallen in love with the enemy. He reached out his hand, saying, "Let's put all this behind us."

Stan took the outstretched hand in a firm handshake. "Please forgive me for making your life miserable. And thank you so much for risking your life to rescue Jan. I'll be forever in your debt."

"I love your sister dearly and it was the least I could do," Richard replied.

Stan flinched at the mention of love, but he made his best effort to smile. "We'll talk about this later. My sister is an honorable woman."

They spent the rest of the evening catching up and making plans.

"I could get fake papers for Jan," Stan said.

"Do you really think he's safe here?" Katrina glanced over while preparing a feast for everyone.

"Why shouldn't he?" Richard asked. Wasn't the family farm the safest place for the boy to be?

"Someone might betray him."

"Oh…"

Stan shook his head. "I don't think that's a problem. Jan was, how old, when they took him to the Ghetto? Eight?"

"Seven years and nine months," Jan answered.

Richard thought the boy must be in a daze to finally be allowed to exist again. He couldn't imagine how a person must feel during eighteen months in hiding, not allowed to be seen, heard, or otherwise noticed.

"It's very improbable that someone would remember let alone recognize him after such a long time. He's changed a lot…" Stan's comment made sense.

"But what do we do with…Agnieska," Katrina whispered

with a fearful glance at the door. None of them had dared to mention her name, but everyone felt the prickling tension in the air. She could knock on the door any minute now – if she'd made it out of the camp.

"Stan, could you go upstairs with Jan and show him his room? He'll sleep with you for the time being," Katrina said.

Stan nodded, and uncle and nephew disappeared upstairs, caught up in cheerful chatting. Katrina had barely finished dinner and set the table with Richard's help when the boy came bolting down the stairs and shouted, "My *ciocia!*"

Katrina rushed toward the front door to see a haggard woman walking up the road to the house. Richard laughed at how Jan weaseled his way past her and launched himself into the other woman's arms.

"Aunt Agni, you're here!" Jan shouted and led her into the house. "You're here. I missed you so much!"

Richard smiled. The boy had been without his aunt for less than twenty-four hours, but it probably had seemed like a lifetime for him.

The Zdanek family kissed and hugged, until Agnieska turned toward Richard. "You must be the brave man the midwife told me about." She took his hand into both of hers and kissed the back of it and said, near to tears, "I'll remain indebted to you for as long as I live for saving Jan and me."

Richard grinned to hide his embarrassment and removed his hand from her grasp. "It was nothing, really."

She opened her mouth to protest, but when her eyes caught his, she seemed to understand and gave a nod. "In any case, thank you."

"How did you get out?" Katrina asked.

"On foot."

Richard could only admire the petite, dark-haired woman who looked like a walking scarecrow. Despite everything, she hadn't lost her humor, and the iron will blazing inside that had enabled her to not only survive years of malnourishment, backbreaking work, crowded living quarters, and disastrous sanitary conditions, but also to hide, feed, and support her nephew throughout that time, ultimately assuring his survival.

Agnieska glanced at Richard as if to ask for his permission to divulge the information. He couldn't see why not and nodded slightly. "Richard here and the midwife somehow got a camp employee uniform and ID card for me, and when the day shift ended, I simply walked out with everyone else. Then I returned everything to Magda and changed into the dress she gave me."

"Dinner is ready," Katrina said, interrupting the story.

"The trouble will begin when you don't show up at the Ghetto tonight." Stan carried an extra chair into the kitchen.

"No one will bother today. But yes, my absence will be noticed in the morning," Agnieska replied.

All the adults looked at each other with awkward faces. Nobody wanted to think about the consequences.

"There's no way they'll connect her escape to us," Katrina finally said.

"I'll get fake papers for both of you, sooner rather than later," Stan offered between big bites of a hearty stew with rabbit meat.

Jan chewed with full cheeks, his shiny eyes revealing that he felt like he was in paradise. Agnieska, though, seemed unable to relax. "We can't stay here. They might come to ask you about my whereabouts and our presence will endanger you."

She had a point there. Once her absence was detected, the police would probably come, interrogating her family.

"You'll stay here until Stan has papers for you," Katrina decided. "If someone visits our house, you hide in the storage room beneath the trap door."

"We know how to hide, right, Jan?"

The boy nodded. "Aunt Agni has been hiding me for one and a half years. Can you imagine? I had to keep quiet all the time and couldn't go outside ever."

Richard's heart broke for the boy. What unimaginable martyrdom for a lively boy Jan's age. After dinner, Agnieska and Jan went upstairs to catch some much-needed sleep. Jan would share the room with Stan, while Agnieska would sleep with Katrina, and Richard had the room to himself. He longed to take Katrina into his arms and feel her soft body against his, showing her how much he'd missed her. He hadn't known her body for so long, but with so many people, especially Stan, in the house, he would have to wait a little longer.

* * *

Stan left before dawn to return to his partisan unit and get papers for Agnieska and Jan. The rest stayed at the farm, living with the threat of discovery breathing down their neck every single moment.

After three days, they relaxed. If the German police hadn't visited by now, they probably wouldn't come. But the fourth day brought an unexpected visitor. Katrina greeted a very agitated Mrs. Koszlow in the hallway.

"Can you imagine that vicious snake?" Mrs. Koszlow clamored and burst into the kitchen.

Richard barely managed to close the trap door, hiding the two Jewish refugees. He couldn't disappear in time, but he needn't have worried. The agitated woman didn't notice him. "She poisoned me. I'm sure of that!"

"Who poisoned you, good woman?" Katrina asked and offered her a seat with the back to Richard.

"Magda Lenska."

Katrina and Richard gasped a breath at the same time, before she motioned for him to sneak out of the kitchen. He waited until Katrina walked over to the sink, pouring water with lemon balm for Mrs. Koszlow. He timed his steps with hers and pressed his back against the wall outside, not daring to escape upstairs for fear he'd make a sound and alarm the woman.

"Here, drink this, it'll refresh you," Katrina said.

The other woman eyed the glass suspiciously. "Are you trying to poison me, too?"

"Me? Of course not." Katrina laughed. "Here, let me drink half of it." She poured half of the water into a second glass and drank it in one gulp.

But Mrs. Koszlow pursed her lips and took only a tiny sip. "As I said, the treacherous snake poisoned me and then she gave my uniform to that ghastly Jewess, who had nothing better to do than to escape with it."

Katrina gasped. "How could that happen?"

"That's why the Jews are our ruin, they have no honest bones in their bodies. They haven't found her yet, but at least this godless midwife has received what's rightfully hers," she spat out, then gave an ugly laugh.

Even from his position in the hallway Richard sensed how Katrina froze at the nasty tone.

"What…what has happened to her?"

"The Gestapo arrested her as soon as I told them what she'd done to me. I imagine she won't be alive for long. Serves her right."

Richard fought the urge to bolt into the kitchen and strangle the vindictive woman. Apparently, Katrina pondered the same idea, because her next words came in a barely controlled voice. "Poor woman."

"Poor woman?" Mrs. Koszlow's voice cackled with rancor. "Do you have the slightest idea what I went through? Having to fear for my job! The Germans initially thought I'd planned the whole thing. Me? Haven't I served them well for the past years? Never complaining about the pay or the long working hours. Don't they think it was hard on me having to deal with all those filthy and disobedient children all the time?"

"Oh yes, you are truly a poor woman. Life has been so hard on you," Katrina said, her voice dripping with false sweetness.

"Well, I try to bear my fate with my head held high. Thanks for the water," the woman said and Richard heard her chair scratch across the wooden planks. He slid into the corner beneath the staircase, thinking it best to avoid her.

Once she'd left the house, Katrina locked the front door behind her and fell into Richard's arms, shaking. Tears streamed down her face as the tension of the past days burst through the dam of her self-control.

"Shush, my darling, she's gone. It's over." His soft words reassured her as he stroked her hair, but he knew it wasn't over yet. It was only a matter of time until the Gestapo made the connection between Agnieska and the Zdaneks. The sooner she and Jan left the farm, the safer for everyone. He prayed Stan would return with fake papers before the Germans came looking for them.

Katrina's sobs faded and he pressed a kiss on her forehead. "Come on, darling. We have to let Agnieska and Jan out of hiding."

"Oh...I totally forgot about them." Katrina slapped a hand across her heart. "Poor Jan. He must have heard every vicious word that woman said. He's so young..."

"He's young, but he's resilient. And in time he'll forget. That's the benefit of youth," Richard said and walked into the kitchen to open the trap door. For himself, he didn't hope for the gift of forgetting. Combat had been an awful experience, but at least after each exhausting battle he'd fallen into a death-like sleep. A few weeks ago, though, the horrors he'd experienced had started haunting him at night. He dreaded falling asleep, because his fallen comrades would visit him in his nightmares, their mouths open in a silent cry, faces disfigured, limbs missing.

He blinked to remove the images and pulled the trapdoor open to release two pale and visibly shaken persons from their confinement.

Much later that evening, when Jan was put asleep upstairs, the three adults sat around the wooden kitchen table.

"Jan and I will leave the moment Stan returns with our

papers," Agnieska said, putting both of her bony hands around a mug of hot herb tea.

"You can't – where will you go?" Katrina asked and Richard's heart squeezed at the pained look in her eyes.

"I still have friends in Warsaw. Gentile friends. With our new papers we can go there and live with them."

Richard knew it was for the best. The new separation would hurt, but with the midwife in the hands of the Gestapo they weren't safe here anymore. Neither was he... nor Katrina. Hot and cold waves shot through his body at the mere thought of his beloved woman in the hands of those brutes. "Katrina and I should leave, too."

Two heads shot around to look at him.

"If the Gestapo tortured Magda, she might have given them my name. Or yours. They may be brutes, but they aren't stupid. They'll make the connection between the midwife, Agnieska, Mrs. Koszlow, and you soon enough."

"I can't leave here, I have to run the farm. Someone has to feed the partisans," Katrina said, pushing her lower lip out.

"Don't you think you'd be of more use to the underground free and alive than in the hands of the Gestapo?" Agnieska put a hand over Katrina's. "I know it's hard to abandon everything you've worked so hard for, but sometimes it is for the best."

"No. And this is my last word." Katrina clonked her mug on the table.

# CHAPTER 27

The next day Stan returned to the family farm with a grin on his face, waving ID cards in his hand.

"Where's Jan?" he asked, scanning the perimeter for the boy.

"Hanging out with Tadzio," Katrina answered. "The two boys have become best friends during these last few days."

"So why do you look as if someone died?" Stan asked after a look at the dreary expressions of the three adults.

"Because someone did...Magda Lenska was caught by the Gestapo and just this morning they found her body hanging from a lamppost in town.

Stan swallowed hard and sat down on a chair. "The good soul. How? Why?"

"Mrs. Koszlow betrayed her," Katrina said through thinned lips.

"That bloody backstabbing bitch!" Stan jumped up, knocking over the chair, and thumped his fist onto the table. "I'll see that she gets what's hers!"

Richard stepped into the doorframe, afraid the large man would bolt out the door this very moment to pay their traitorous neighbor an unpleasant visit. "Don't. She's not worth it."

Stan stared at him with bloodshot eyes. "You in cahoots with her, Fritz?"

"No. Never. And I thought we'd left the hostilities behind?"

Stan gave an unintelligible grunt, but backed up.

"You can have your revenge on Mrs. Koszlow later, but first we have to bring everyone to a safe place. In fact Agnieska and Jan will leave today for Warsaw, now that you've obtained papers for them. Katrina and I should leave the farm as well–" Richard explained.

"And since when are you the boss here?"

"Since I'm the only one thinking with a clear head. And before you get all riled up, I was hoping for your help to convince that stubborn lady over there," he said, pointing to Katrina, "to leave the farm, since it's not safe here anymore."

Stan shook his head and ran his hand through his hair. Once, twice, three times. "Richard is right. The Gestapo will find out that Agnieska is our sister-in-law and then none of us will be safe here. They may even believe we had nothing to do with it, but they might still arrest us just for fun. To fill their pool of hostages for reprisal shootings."

Katrina blanched. The private war staged between the Home Army and the SS had taken on absurd dimensions. For every assassination of one German man, ten to twenty Polish civilians were shot. Usually a roundup happened in town, and whichever male Pole had the bad luck to be out and about would be shot later. But the Gestapo also liked to help out their SS friends by providing a pool of hostages to use for reprisals. Most of them might actually be grateful for the quick end after being held captive for days or weeks in the Gestapo's hands.

"I'm not leaving. I have to supply food to the partisans."

"Think again, sister," Stan pleaded with her. "You can be of more use to us alive than dead or in a German labor camp. You can go to Bartosz's farm. Since he and his two brothers are in hiding, his mother could use a hand...or two," he said after a glance at Richard.

"And who will take care of our place?" Katrina spoke out aloud what nobody wanted to think about.

"We'll worry about this another day. For now Tadzio and his ma can do the most urgent things here." Stan turned to look at Agnieska. "Pack your things. I might be able to get you on a horse-drawn cart to Warsaw, but it has to be first thing in the morning. We'll leave in thirty."

Frantic activity ensued in the small cottage. Agnieska packed the few belongings she owned – mostly dresses Katrina had given her for herself, and a few trousers and shirts Tadzio had outgrown. The neighbor's boy might be the same age as Jan, but four years of starvation were clearly reflected in their difference of stature.

Katrina prepared cold snacks for the journey and two blankets for the nights, and finally she dipped her fingers deep into the flour pot and produced a few zloty notes and a small golden ring.

"I can't possibly take this," Agnieska protested.

"Yes, you can. It was Ludmila's wedding band. It'll serve you well to start a new life in Warsaw."

"Thank you." Agnieska took the band and stashed it in a secret pocket of her dress, as her eyes filled with tears. She quickly turned away, pretending to be busy rearranging the clothes in her satchel.

Tadzio and Jan came running toward the farm, cheeks red, hair ruffled. Breathless, Jan jumped at his uncle Stan, calling, "I have to show you something, come..."

"We can't." Stan kneeled beside the boy. "We have to leave right now. It's not safe to stay here. Say good-bye to Tadzio."

Jan's eyes watered but he braved the threat of tears and nodded before he hugged his friend good-bye. "We'll see each other after the war. Wait for me?"

"Sure, I'll wait. Don't worry. I'll keep the bloody Germans off this place." Tadzio raised his fists into the air, and Richard couldn't hold back a grin.

Before Stan left with Agnieska and the boy, he turned to Richard and said, "Have everything packed by tomorrow night. I'll be back with someone to give you and Katrina a ride to Bartosz's farm."

"Thanks, Stan." As he shared a comradely glance with Stan, Richard realized he didn't have anything to fear from Katrina's brother. The larger man had come around and accepted him into the family.

Then Katrina and Richard were alone. After so many days when the cottage had been filled with chatter and laughter, the silence seemed unfamiliar.

"I miss them already," Katrina said.

"Me too, but look at the bright side. I finally get to share your bed again."

She flushed and looked away. "How can you think of that now?"

But the next moment she was in his arms and he carried her up the stairs. "God, I missed you so much, Katrina."

He settled her onto the bed and kissed her cheek lightly, raising her face up to look at him. Then he pressed his lips on hers. He felt her body yielding to him as he deepened the kiss, his hands slipping beneath her dress and up her thighs, roaming over her hips, her stomach, and the swell of her breasts.

"I love you, Richard," Katrina whispered, as she raised her arms for him to rid her of the dress. "I'm the luckiest woman in the world to have you back with me."

They took the whole night to relearn each other's bodies. When they finally fell asleep, Richard hoped with Katrina in his arms the nightmares would leave him alone. Inhaling her sweet scent, he dozed off, praying the warmth of her skin pressed against his would keep him grounded in the here and now.

Nonetheless, the nightmares attacked him and he woke up, sweating and shivering. Katrina still lay by his side, breathing evenly, so he hoped she hadn't noticed his inner turmoil. He would not burden her with his problems. Shell shock they called it. Or battle fatigue. It usually didn't start until after the war – at least that's how it had been in the previous war.

He slid his hand across her wonderful curves and snuggled tighter against her. As long as she was with him, he'd overcome his nightmares – one day. He might even be able to forget.

The next morning Katrina gave Tadzio instructions on how to care for the remaining rabbits and the vegetable garden. They would take half of the rabbits plus the hens with them to Bartosz's farm, since she didn't want to arrive as supplicants.

Tadzio put on a brave face and then left through the backyard to cross the fields. He'd just reached the hedge serving as boundary when he came rushing back, waving his hands in the air and shouting, "German soldiers."

"Shit!" Richard said as he saw the motorized vehicle dashing down the dirt road, leaving a cloud of dust in the air. With screeching brakes it came to a halt in front of the farmhouse, and Richard waved for Tadzio to sneak away to his own place.

The next moment loud banging threatened to burst the front door. Richard rushed inside, even though he knew he should go into hiding. But hiding wouldn't help. He'd seen the soldiers and they must have seen him, too. It was better to act normal, hear out what they had to say.

Katrina had already opened the door to a group of SS men who rumbled inside with their heavy boots, leaving clumps of mud on the immaculate kitchen floor. With relief, Richard noticed that he'd never seen any one of them before.

"How can I help you?" Katrina asked with a solemn face, but Richard could see the anxiety in her rigid posture, and her hand grasping the table. Despite the severe situation, his heart filled with warmth looking at the valiant woman he loved so much. Like always, she refused to talk German to the occupiers, but they'd come prepared. Two of the men were Blue Police, and one of them addressed her in Polish. "Where's your sister-in-law?"

Katrina pushed out her lower lip and glared daggers at the one speaking. "Shouldn't you know that, Aleksy? It was you who dragged her to the Ghetto years ago."

"Don't play innocent with me, Katrina. She escaped and we know she came here."

"I haven't seen her since the day you took her," Katrina said. Her lie was compelling enough to swipe the smug grin from Aleksy's face as he turned to translate her words for the SS.

"We don't believe you," Aleksy finally said and the German officer, whom Richard recognized to be an SS Untersturmführer by the collar badge and shoulder straps, waved at his men, shouting, "Search the place! Every single corner. If you find so much as a trace of the missing Jewess, tear her into pieces, and this one, too." Most of the men sped into all corners of the cottage, leaving only the commanding officer, the Blue policeman called Aleksy, and another SS man holding his rifle at the ready in the kitchen.

The officer took a step toward Katrina, taking her chin between thumb and forefinger, raising his hand until she barely touched the ground with her tiptoes. "You know what the punishment for hiding Jews is?"

Seeing Katrina fighting for breath, Richard couldn't hold back any longer. He stepped forward and said in German, laced heavily with a Polish accent, "Officer, please let her go. We're hiding no Jew."

"And who are you? Never seen you here before," the Blue policeman called Aleksy asked.

"Ri...Ryszard Blach, I'm Katrina's cousin," Richard said, remembering to use his made-up identity.

"Papers," the German officer demanded.

"I...I don't have them anymore. My home burnt out during an air raid and everything with it." Richard shivered inside at his weak excuse, but he didn't have a better one at his fingertips. Why hadn't he asked Stan to put together fake papers for him as well? That negligence might now cost him his life.

"Hmm." The German officer let Katrina's jaw go and she tumbled to the floor, then scrambled to get up again. He glanced at her like she was a mangy dog and kicked her with his muddy boot. Richard could barely restrain himself from jumping at the officer's throat. A sure death sentence, and not only for him. So he gritted his teeth and looked away.

"Get out of my sight, filthy bitch," the officer commanded and launched another kick at her ribs for good measure. She stifled a scream and crawled away until she reached the back door.

"Not so fast," the officer said when she wanted to open the door. "Now for you," he drawled, taking his sweet time walking around Richard, inspecting him from all sides. "Not a Jew," he murmured and then came to stand in front of Richard again. "Are you sure you're not a *Volksdeutscher* who has failed to register? That is punishable by death."

Richard swallowed hard. He'd never heard of that specific law, but then, what did it matter? The officer had all the power to make up these things, and who would complain? Certainly not a frightened-to-death Polish peasant. "Officer, no. If I were a *Volksdeutscher* I would most definitely have registered."

"How old are you?"

"Almost nineteen."

"Well, well," the officer said with a dirty grin, "congratulations, you've just joined the ranks of the SS. The Dirlewanger brigade."

"No...Officer..." Richard felt all the blood rushing from his face. Not that. Never. He'd rather be shot.

"Your choice." The officer pointed at Katrina, who still stood beside the back door, shivering like aspen leaves. "You fight for the Reich or this piece of ass will serve in the brothel in town. We're always short of willing girls."

"I'd rather fight, then..." Richard said.

"Too bad, and here I was looking forward to getting down and dirty with your cousin. Maybe you'd like to watch?"

Richard fisted his hands. If the SS officer so much as laid a hand on Katrina, he'd strangle him with his bare hands, even if it were the last thing he'd do in this life.

"Untersturmführer, we found nothing," one of the returning SS troopers said, as eight or ten of the men trampled into the kitchen. A short discussion ensued and some of the men turned the kitchen upside down to look for valuables in the drawers.

"We are outta here then. He's coming with us, joining the war effort, and the girl..." The officer glanced around, but Katrina had used the hullabaloo to slip through the door, begging Richard's pardon with her last glance before she dashed off towards Tadzio's house.

The soldiers frogmarched Richard to the military

vehicle as he worried what the sadistic Dirlewanger had in store for him should he recognize him. But his worries were soon overshadowed when he saw one of the SS troopers light a bundle of straw stalks and torch the thatched roof of the farmhouse.

Time stood still as Richard prayed this was just another of his harrowing nightmares.

CHAPTER 28

M anhandled into the flatbed truck, Richard crouched in a corner, his eyes watering at the sight of black smoke hovering in the sky over the farm. After a while, the truck passed through a tiny village.

"Stop!" someone shouted. "I'm hungry." The other men joined in a raucous laugh. "And thirsty," another one yelled. Cigarettes were lit and a solicitous man pushed one between Richard's lips after he tied him to the truck saying, "Wait here. Be right back."

All men jumped from the truck and swarmed out to the houses of the villagers, pillaging for food and booze. Their commanding officer made no attempt to stop them, but leaned back in the driver's cabin and stuffed a pipe.

Richard tried to free his hands, but to no avail. The SS trooper had clearly immobilized a prisoner before. Knocking his head against the rear wall of the driver's cabin in despair, Richard drew on his cigarette. He'd stopped smoking since living with Katrina, but now he was grateful for the raspy feeling in his throat. The cig would soon numb the hunger starting to rumble in his belly.

An hour or two later, the SS men returned with sated expressions on their faces. A few of them held booty in their hands in the form of bottles of vodka. They filled the truck, pushing and shoving for the best place.

"Hey you, Polacke, get out of my way," someone said.

"I would, if you'd loosen the rope around my hands," Richard answered.

The other one glanced at him and nodded. "Know what? Try to run and we make it a competition of how many bullets you can take before you die."

"Understood."

The truck started up again and with the rumbling and jolting on the dirt road, Richard was glad he could use his hands to soften the blows. Suddenly the truck came to a screeching halt, the driver cursing. Everyone jumped out, oblivious to their prisoner, appraising the damage. A huge trunk lay across the street, effectively blocking the passage.

Richard low-crawled to the edge of the bed when a sooty face with dark brown eyes stared at him.

He'd never been happier to see his nemesis.

"Get out," Stan hissed.

Richard didn't need to be asked twice. He slipped off the flatbed and followed Stan a few dozen yards into the woods, where a horse grazed. Richard's eyes went wide as Stan mounted the horse, extended his hand, and said, "Hop on."

Seconds later he came to sit behind Stan – how, he had no idea – and clung to Katrina's brother for dear life as the horse galloped into the woods. After an endless ride, when Richard's legs and behind went numb, the crazy horse finally stopped and Richard all but dropped down onto safe non-moving ground.

"Wasn't that bad, was it, green-face?" Stan grinned at him and dismounted too.

Richard flopped against a trunk, turning his focus to regaining equilibrium. Who'd have thought that riding a horse was akin to mounting a roller coaster? A few minutes later he finally found his voice again. "Thanks for saving my life, Stan."

"Nothing to speak of." Stan made a dismissive gesture, although both of them knew it was indeed something to speak of.

"How'd you know?"

"Wasn't hard to guess. The smoke column stood high in the sky and I rushed to the farm, but too late. The roof's destroyed and flames licking at the wooden beams. Will all be gone by now." Stan grimaced. The farmhouse had withstood wind and weather for over a hundred years – until looting SS bastards came to call.

"Katrina?" Richard's breath caught in his throat as he waited for the answer. Relief spread through his veins as a grin spread across Stan's face.

"Fine. You still much in love with her, Fritz?" Stan uttered the insult with appreciation rather than spite.

"Always will be. She's a fine woman and I can't imagine ever having to live without her."

Stan gave an exaggerated sigh, saying, "I guess there's nothing I can do then. Here she comes."

The sound of clattering horse's hooves became louder and then stopped. A horse-drawn cart stood several yards away on a beaten track Richard hadn't noticed before.

Katrina jumped out and flew into his arms, almost knocking him over.

"Darling, sweetheart, you're here. You're alive." She showered him with kisses, before she let him go and turned to her brother, who held up his hands to keep her from doing the same to him. "Stan. I'll never forget what you did." Tears started rolling down her face and both men fought with their own emotions.

"Come on, I don't have all day," someone called from the coach box.

"That's Bartosz. He'll give us a ride to his farm," Katrina said and used a moment of Stan's abstraction to sling her arms around her brother's neck. "Thank you so much, Stan. I know how you hated Richard, therefore I'm all the more grateful that you rescued him."

"Get on the cart," Stan ordered and wriggled out of her embrace, visibly embarrassed at her outburst of emotions. Then he turned to Richard. "Take good care of her, hear me?"

"You know I'd protect her with my own life."

Stan nodded. "Better do that. If you ever hurt her, I'll have to come and finish what your compatriots started."

"No need," Richard said with a chuckle. "Take care of yourself. I hope this war ends soon and we can all get back to our lives." He knew it wouldn't be that easy, and he also knew that nobody could just go on with their lives as if nothing had happened. But he hoped for a fresh start – with Katrina. Without glancing backwards, he climbed on the horse-drawn cart where Katrina already waited for him amidst the things she'd managed to salvage from the farmhouse before it had burnt to the ground.

The journey took several hours and Richard stretched out on his back, holding the woman he loved so much in his arms, the rocking and swaying cart making it almost a romantic ride, if it hadn't been for the cackling hens and squeaking rabbits.

"I hope we survive this wretched war. I look forward to seeing my family," Richard said, looking up into the sky. "And, I look forward to being together with you in peaceful times."

"Well, I'll have to give that a lot of thought," she teased him even as she snuggled up against his side.

Warmth spread from his heart throughout his entire body and he couldn't wait one second longer. He turned to look at her and asked, "Katrina Zdanek, will you marry me?"

She giggled with delight and pressed a kiss on his lips before she replied, "Yes. Yes. Yes. I would marry you this very moment if I could, Richard Klausen."

"We have to wait until all of this is over," he cautioned her, but she already started daydreaming.

"I imagine my family and yours being together, getting to know each other. I want to meet your sisters, your parents, even the aunt you told me about. Everyone. When there's peace we can travel to visit them in Berlin or they could come here and spend their vacation with us. I want to restore the cottage and farm one day, become a healer like my parents were. Do you think you can live there, my darling?"

"I will live wherever you live, my love. I kind of grew fond of the country life. It's hard work, but I have big plans for our future, too. Perhaps I could open a school and teach the children literature. Finer education has been neglected much too long in both of our countries," Richard said.

"As long as both of us have time for our home and family." Katrina sighed. "I want to have lots of little Klausens running about the place. What do you think of that?"

"I think you sometimes have great ideas, my beloved darling," Richard replied and wrapped his arms tighter around her shoulders.

* * *

Thank you for taking the time to read TROUBLE BREWING. If you enjoyed this book and are feeling generous, please leave me a review.

You'll meet some of the characters again in the next book, FATAL ENCOUNTER.

Lotte Klausen and her Polish brother-in-law Piotr Zdanek are both in Warsaw on the eve of the Uprising – on opposing sides.

When they meet during the heat of the battle will they be able to spare each other's lives or does the war between their countries tear the family apart?

Pre-order here:
http://kummerow.info/book/fatal-encounter

Thanks so much for your support!

# AUTHOR'S NOTES

D ear Reader,

Thanks so much for reading TROUBLE BREWING. When I started the War Girl series, I never planned for Richard to get his own book. Since he was away at the front, I thought he'd simply stay there.

But my characters like to surprise me and usually don't do the things I expect them to. So Richard stubbornly weaseled his way into my head, demanding his own book. It was a tough book to write, because it was the first time I had a soldier as my main character and that was new territory for me.

Talking about soldiers: Johann Hauser, Richard's squad leader in Lodz, started out as a minor character, but he begged me to appear in another book. His wish was granted and you'll meet him again in the next book in the War Girl series, Fatal Encounter.

But there's even more exciting things happening with Johann. He'll make a cameo appearance as young man before the war in Shanghai Story, a WWII drama written by my friend Alexa Kang. I, for one, cannot wait until I can get my hands on her book.

After my visit to Warsaw, Poland in June 2017 I wanted to set this story in Warsaw, but much to my dismay found out, that the Warsaw Ghetto had been liquidated already in Spring 1943, long before Richard even arrived in Poland.

Thankfully, my research unearthed that there was one single Ghetto left in Poland to exist until June 1944, which was in Lodz, so I moved the story there. The correct spelling of the city is Łódź, but for ease of reading I use the English form Lodz.

Even today, the head of the Council of Elders, Chaim Rudowski, is one of the most controversial figures of occupied Poland. He transformed the Ghetto into a productivity machine manufacturing war supplies for the Wehrmacht, because he believed that being useful to the Germans would ensure the survival of the Ghetto occupants. Whether he really believed this or seized the opportunity for his own wealth and power, is not clear.

Rudowski will always be remembered for his speech "Give me your children". In the story, the midwife Magda recalls his speech. It must have been beyond moving for anyone present there, especially the parents who were asked to send their children into death.

Attached to the Ghetto was the Kinder KZ, and while officially the minimum age was eight years, the youngest prisoner of the camp was a boy of two years and three months. Petty offences like stealing food, loitering in the streets, or even the fact that the children were orphans easily became resons to send them to the camp.

By the way, Lodz is also the place, where the parents of my father-in-law lived before the war. At that time the city had a huge population of Germans and many people in the area were bilingual.

The village of Baluty is just a random village I chose for the story, but massacres like the one I described have happened across Poland and Russia.

Oskar Dirlewanger was a real person and from my research, he was even more reproachable in reality than I depicted him in the book. The incident where Richard was supposed to shoot the unarmed and wounded Pole actually happened in during the Warsaw Uprising, as testified by the eighteen year old soldier Matthias Schenk.

Of course I couldn't have written this book without the help of so many special people. Many thanks go to Anja Matijczak and her mother who checked the Polish words and dishes for correctness.

And as always I want to thank my fantastic cover designer Daniela Colleo from stunningbookcovers.com. I'd been wanting to do a cover with this particular model for ages and finally the perfect story came along and she made the perfect cover for it.

Tami Stark, my editor, and Martin O'Hearn my proof-reader made this book the best it can be by clening up typos, unclear sentences, or anachronistic terms.

More thanks go to JJ Toner, an author of Second World War Fiction himself who generously offered to beta-read Trouble Brewing.

I couldn't have done without the help of all these wonderful people!

But my acknowledgements wouldn't be complete, without mentioning you, my reader! Thank you for all the support, your wonderful emails, the encouragement, and the kind words. I love hearing from you!

If you're seeking a group of wonderful people who have an interest in WWII fiction, you are more than welcome to join our Facebook group.

https://www.facebook.com/groups/962085267205417

Again, I want to thank you from the bottom of my heart for taking the time to read my book and if you liked it (or even if you didn't) I would appreciate a sincere review.

Marion Kummerow

Manufactured by Amazon.ca
Bolton, ON

13301290R00116